The Heart to Live

A Novel

Shauna Jamieson Carty

Island Novel
Divine Word Communications, LLC, *Roselle, New Jersey*

SHAUNA JAMIESON CARTY

The Heart to Live
A Novel

Copyright © 2018 by Shauna Jamieson Carty
All rights reserved.

This novel was first published in 2010 under the title
Cover Me: The College Years, by Jamieson Carty

No part of this book may be used or reproduced or transmitted in any form or by any means--electronic or mechanical, including photocopying, recording, or by any information storage and retrieval system--without the written permission of the publisher, except in the case of brief quotations and as otherwise provided by the United States of America copyright law.

Island Novel Publishing is a division of Divine Word Communications, LLC, a publisher and promoter of Christian literature. Our products can be purchased in bulk at a discounted price. Please contact us for details at prayerpartnersnovels@yahoo.com.

This book is a work of fiction. All of the characters, names, incidents, organizations and dialogues in this novel are either the products of the author's imagination or are used in a fictitious manner.

Scriptures are taken from the New King James Version of the Bible. Copyright © 1982 by Thomas Nelson, Inc. Used by permission. All rights reserved. Old English verses are taken from the King James Version.

Printed in the United States of America

ISBN: **099164333X**
ISBN-13: **978-0-9916433-3-2**

THE HEART TO LIVE

DEDICATION

I dedicate this book to God who is love (1 John 4:8), to the love of my life Ricky who God blessed me to love and marry, to our five children who God is blessing us to nurture and love, and to my mother who has always inspired me with her love.

BOOKS IN THE
PRAYER PARTNERS SERIES

The Heart to Love
By Shauna Jamieson Carty

When a teenage boy says he has the heart to love a girl for the rest of their lives, can she believe him? Wendy's mother believed Wendy's father and ended up pregnant and alone. Now Wendy is 17 years old and saving herself for her high school sweetheart Paul. Paul promises to marry her after graduation and enter a covenant of everlasting love. Wendy's mother withholds her blessings and cautions them to wait. Now Wendy is about to find out where her father stands: beside her as she walks down the aisle or by her mother.

The Heart to Live
By Shauna Jamieson Carty

College life isn't the "happily ever after" that Wendy and Paul dreamed of when they were in high school. They attend the same university, but nothing seems to be going according to their plans. "Remember to pray for me," Paul tells Wendy. Wendy covers Paul with her prayers, but their security is shattered and depression sets in because of a tragic shooting on their college campus. Will sharing their faith help to restore the peace and give them and their peers the heart to live joyfully again?

The Heart to Forgive
By Shauna Jamieson Carty

Love is everlasting, except of course when our loved ones hurt our feelings and it's just too hard to forgive. At the center of Paul and Wendy's faith is the belief that they can pray to God and ask for forgiveness for the things they have done wrong. God will forgive them and they must forgive others. They and their friends Constance and Sergio pursue different paths after college, but they share a common loss and continue to get together for a memorial benefit concert once a year. Can they get past the pain of hurtful relationships? Will they have the heart to forgive themselves and each other and embrace God's unfailing love?

Dear Readers:

Thank you for spending time with us. I pray that your faith in God has been built up as you read the Prayer Partners Series of novels.

The Lord gave me the vision for the three novels in this series many years ago, and it took many years and many stages to manifest. This novel was first published under the title, Cover Me: The College Years, by Jamieson Carty. This is the same story, with minor corrections, under the new title The Heart to Live in order to make the series more unified. To God be the glory! Praise the Lord! Alleluia! Thank you, JESUS!

Submit your relationships to God, seek His forgiveness, and trust Him to reconcile broken hearts.

"Now all things are of God, who has reconciled us to Himself through Jesus Christ, and has given us the ministry of reconciliation, that is, that God was in Christ reconciling the world to Himself, not imputing their trespasses to them, and has committed to us the word of reconciliation." (2 Corinthians 5:18-19 NKJV)

Please write to us at prayerpartnersnovels@gmail.com; we'd love to hear from you.

Peace, love, and God bless,

Shauna

THE HEART TO LIVE

ACKNOWLEDGMENTS

Praise the Lord! Alleluia! Thank you, JESUS!

Thank you to my mommy who set an unforgettable example for me as a writer when she typed her first 500-page manuscript on a typewriter on the back verandah of our home on the island of Jamaica. *Centre of the Labyrinth*, by Rosetta J. Jamieson is still my favorite novel.

Thanks to my husband Ricky for believing that I should use this gift of writing that the Lord has placed in me and for supporting me in doing so every step of the way.

Thanks to our children for cheering me on, for reading my work, and for the many writing projects of their own that I love to read.

Thank God for my church family at Second Baptist Church in Roselle, New Jersey, and for all the people who remember me and my family in their prayers. "...The effective, fervent prayer of a righteous man avails much." (James 5:16)

Thanks to my cover models who inspired me and became wind beneath my wings as we worked on this project.

Special thanks to my sister in Christ, Pauline Finley, for expecting nothing less than three novels in this series.

Thanks to biblegateway.com and all the other Bible references on the Internet that make it easy to find a scripture for every moment of our lives.

CHAPTER ONE

The door to the auditorium swung open just as Wendy Douglas reached for the doorknob.

"Wendy!" Paul Chambers let the door slam shut behind him as he stood face to face with the only girl who had ever broken his heart. Instinctively, he held her hands for a moment, drawn by the love he still felt for her. Then, he let his hands drop beside him.

"It's good to see you, Paul. How are you?"

"I'm good," he replied, unable and unwilling to tell her that her mere presence filled him up. He wouldn't tell anyone about the subtle confirmation he felt, the feeling of completeness he had always felt whenever she was around.

Wendy sighed as he stepped aside, relieved that he had put some breathing room between their bodies. In the next breath, she could feel her body temperature rise as she realized he was checking her out.

Paul checked her out slowly, admiring her hair, face, and body. He noticed the deep dark tan she'd acquired, probably from lying out on the beach at her father's hotel in Jamaica over the summer. Her complexion glowed against the orange leotard that hugged her upper body. A long, voluminous skirt clung to her waistline, flared at her hips, and ballooned around her ankles.

"You look good. I don't need to ask how you are," he observed.

Wendy grinned. She couldn't hide the fact that she was happy to see him. It pleased her that they'd bumped into each other like this. It delighted her that he was taking the time to talk to her. The connection between them had always been such that in one look, they could see beyond the superficial exterior to the inner workings of each other's mind.

Their lifelong friendship meshed two souls, united by their love for each other and for God. They had made plans to marry each other at the end of their senior year of high school. They used to say back then that it was God's plan for their life: marriage, living together while they attended the same college, and moving to Africa to work as missionaries after graduation. Instead, after their high school graduation, they broke up. Paul was heartbroken when Wendy spent that summer in Africa without him. He went ahead of her to college and started dating someone else.

It had hurt Wendy deeply to watch Paul and his new girlfriend spend time together over the last two years, but now as Paul looked intently into her eyes, Wendy felt a renewed sense of hope. She saw love there, beyond the hurt and anger he'd felt when she had gone off to Africa two summers ago without him, using a plane ticket she bought with her daddy's money.

"It's good to be back for another semester," she said. "Can you believe we're already in our junior year?"

"Believe it," Paul replied, simply enjoying her company.

"Oh yeah! My parents send their congratulations on the release of your second CD."

Paul chuckled. "Thanks. Who knew your father would turn out to be a prophet?"

"You're an amazing musician and singer, Paul. A career in music was yours for the taking. All you had to do was want it."

The admiration Paul saw in her eyes stripped away the years. Like her, he was approaching his twentieth birthday, but her compliment took him back to a time when they were little children. They were close friends, way back then, as they grew up together in church. She prayed him through overcoming his shyness to becoming a youth leader and musical director in their church. In return, he'd encouraged her to sing.

They'd grown up playing and praying together. By the time they were teenagers, they'd pledged their hearts. First, they promised they would honor the Lord by waiting until after they got married to become intimately involved. Then, they promised their bodies to each other.

"You always believed in me," Paul stated, tilting his head slightly toward her. "Thank you."

"Daddy is like your biggest fan. He still plays the CD we made when we were in high school. You know, the time we went with my parents to the amusement park."

"As if I could ever forget," Paul replied. "It was your father's birthday."

"Yes, it was Daddy's birthday. I'm happy you remember."

Paul remembered that trip to the amusement park quite well. He had been penniless back then, and even though he prayed hard about it, he'd resented each time Wendy's father flaunted his money.

Wendy and Paul had grown up with single mothers in New York. They both experienced the inadequacy of their mother's income and longed for their father to protect and provide for them.

Wendy met her father for the first time during her final year of high school, and after her parents got married, she formally started using her father's last name. Paul felt like her father gradually nudged him aside by showering Wendy with his presence and more presents than she knew what to do with. Wendy's father had transformed Wendy's life as much as Paul's music career was now transforming his.

Wendy continued, "Of course, the CD we made became his most prized possession when you received a Stellar and a Dove award for the best new artist. I still have my copy."

Paul stared intently into Wendy's eyes as she spoke. He hadn't forgotten anything about their relationship. The closeness they shared surpassed any relationship he ever had with another person, or ever expected to have. If only she'd waited for them to travel to Africa together as they'd planned. By the time she returned, he'd made up his mind not to allow her to get close to him again. He couldn't help the fact that he loved her more than he'd ever loved anyone else, but he wouldn't give her the chance to abandon him ever again.

"My parents were really disappointed when you didn't come to their wedding. Dad said he hoped you would remember the little people."

That comment could have made Paul mad, but instead, his sense of humor kicked in. "I would hardly call Daddy Big-Bucks little people," he retorted. "I've seen the ads for his villa resort and hotel. Come home to Jamaica. No problem, man. Enjoy we beautiful island."

Wendy laughed out loud at his sorry imitation of a Jamaican accent and at his body language. As Paul spoke, he opened his arms wide and gyrated his hips—a silly-looking posture for a slender guy who was over six feet tall. Vintage Paul. Hilarious. Wendy missed being around him. Throughout high school, they'd been inseparable. They had been best friends for all but the last two years of her life, and he used to constantly bring laughter to her lips, even during the most painful moments.

She'd never get over him. She didn't want to. Sharing this moment with him confirmed her belief that she would win him back. Life hadn't gone according to what they used to think was God's plan. Perhaps, it was better this way, not to have married each other right after high school. They'd been living on the same college campus for the last two years, but they spent most of their time with other people. Perhaps, in the long run, that experience would strengthen them individually, and make them better partners for each other once they resumed their relationship.

"I love you." She longed to say those words to him as their laughter quieted.

The auditorium doors flew open. "Paul. Honey. I can't believe you're standing out here. The show is about to begin." Constance Victoria

Channing grabbed hold of his hand.

Paul shifted his attention from Wendy to the young woman standing next to him, tugging on his arm. She rivaled Wendy in height and body structure; but where Wendy's skin tone evoked chocolate, Constance's conjured up creamy caramel.

He apologized to Constance. "I'm sorry. I lost track of time. I'm going to run to the car now..."

"No, baby," Constance shifted his chin with her left hand and kissed Paul lightly on the lips, before shooting daggers at Wendy with her eyes. "I asked Georgia to get my bag for me, once she got through exclaiming over my engagement ring." Constance spoke loudly and held her hand up in front of her for emphasis. She achieved the effect she was aiming for, as other college students swarmed the couple.

"Oh my goodness! You guys got engaged!" A group of Constance's sorority sisters flocked them, squealing with excitement.

Paul tried to see pass them to Wendy, but she was no longer standing nearby. He didn't see whether she had gone inside the auditorium, or back out onto the playing field, but he knew she would be hurting. He should have told her while they were standing there. He was sorry that she'd found out this way. It was like he'd forgotten about Constance while he stood there talking to Wendy. As their peers crowded the area outside of the auditorium and passed freely in and out of the doors, he had ignored all the activity and had given her his undivided attention. Now, she was gone. Undoubtedly, she would be hurt by his lack of explanation that Constance was no longer just his girlfriend. She was his fiancée.

CHAPTER TWO

"Wendy!"

She heard her friend Kim's voice in the distance as she tried to run away.

"Where are you going, girl? Get over here. Donna wants to make one last change to our dance routine."

"No way," Wendy replied, surprised at the commanding sound of her voice. "Donna, this isn't just a dance routine. We prayed about this. Remember? And as we choreographed the dance, we all had a chance to meditate on Psalm 91."

"Yeah. I know. I know." Donna rolled her eyes. She considered herself to be a Christian. That's why she had joined the liturgical dance group on campus. But she was a dance major and had ideas that Wendy was not giving her a chance to express. She understood that the song they were going to dance to had lyrics that were based on a Bible verse, but it had a reggae beat, and to her that meant their moves should be more brassy. "I just don't see how we're going to win the talent show with these angelic moves."

"It's not about winning," Wendy responded. "God's word never returns void, remember? It's about bringing a Bible message to a secular environment."

Donna shook her head and laughed to herself. No wonder Wendy had earned the name Holy Roller.

"What?" Wendy demanded.

"I'm saying though." Donna paused.

"What?" Wendy sounded uncharacteristically mean, uncompromising, and angry.

"Nothing." Donna decided not to challenge her. They were friends: she, Wendy and Kim. Besides, Donna could guess what was wrong. As she and Kim had watched Wendy running away from the auditorium, and away from the playing field where the club fair was being set up, they guessed that she'd heard. The news about Paul and Constance's engagement had spread through the crowd like wildfire. They knew Wendy would be devastated. Donna was impressed by the way she was holding up. She smiled at her. "I like how you're handling it."

"Handling what?" Wendy asked, her voice sounded gentler now.

"The dance, the choreography, everything."

"Pray for me, please," Wendy whispered, squeezing her eyes shut.

Both Donna and Kim reached for her hands.

"Right on time, here come the other girls." Kim gestured to them to hurry over.

They formed a circle of six and prayed. In the midst of the sounds of Hip Hop blaring from the speakers, the laughter, the squeals, and the shouts emanating from among the swarm of college students gathered at the annual club fair, the six girls from Wendy's liturgical dance team got alone with their God.

Wendy was thankful that each took a turn saying a prayer. She needed the time to reign in her emotions. She had gasped sharply the moment she noticed the engagement ring on Constance's finger. When Constance declared that Paul was her fiancé, Wendy felt like her heart stopped. Even now, she willed herself to breath normally. She didn't hear the words prayed by the other members of the dance team. Their voices were drowned out by the thudding of her aching heart.

"Lord, help me, Jesus!" Not a sound left her lips. She sealed them as tightly shut as her eyelids, like levees holding back a dam filled with tears.

"Hallelujah!" The girls lifted their linked hands, signaling the end of their prayer, and that they were ready to perform.

"Hallelujah!" Wendy repeated, as she opened her eyes and smiled. She knew that the strength she was running on now was not her own.

The girls took their places behind a table they had set up with flyers and brochures. They shared the space with the Christian students' club. Lining both sides of an expansive playing field were more tables with paraphernalia from the college's myriad of student organizations. The choices reflected the students' interest in fraternities, sororities, religious organizations, athletic teams, academic societies, career associations, sexual awareness clubs, talent troupes, cultural groups, and politics. This year, as usual, the campus would host its student government elections, but it was the national elections that harnessed most of the students' interest in politics.

For the first time in American history, an African American was representing the Democratic Party. Students rallied behind Barack Obama, a senator from Illinois, whose campaign wooed young people in a way no other politician ever had before. The Obama campaign tapped into the technology of the day, using text messaging and e-mail to connect with students who were just coming of age to vote.

From his position by the table for the African and American Students Union, Sergio Rayford snapped shut his cell phone and kept his eyes on Wendy—although the girls flocking him probably didn't notice. Raising both hands to his head, he lifted his long heavy dreadlocks and moved his head from side to side relaxing the muscles of his neck. A female standing next to him ran her fingers across his shoulders.

"I could give you a massage later tonight," she whispered, leaning toward his ear.

In vintage Sergio style, he undressed the long legged, curvy supermodel type with his eyes.

She smiled back at him and winked.

He licked his lips, but stopped short of saying, "I just might take you up on that offer."

Sergio was a player. He loved women, and he had more offers than he could handle for the taking. That was the third proposal in less than an hour, from women in the same group who were friends with each other.

"Did each one not know what the other was suggesting to him?" he wondered.

He chuckled and shook his head, before letting his eyes wander back to Wendy. He watched the rest of the dancers pray and noticed that Wendy hadn't said anything.

"Freaks," someone at Sergio's table uttered derisively, gesturing toward Wendy and her friends.

"Religious fanatics," agreed another.

"Whatever happened to praying in the secret place? Spirituality is supposed to be a private matter."

Sergio made eye contact with the female beside him as she made the last comment. He heard her final statement and had to consciously stop himself from silencing her with Wendy's typical response. He could hear Wendy's voice in his head defending her right to pray in public, as she had on so many occasions in the two years since he'd met her.

They had met each other in Africa during the summer before Wendy started her freshman year in college. He had already completed his first year of college and had won a scholarship to study abroad. He chose to go to Ghana. Wendy was there alone visiting a host family and doing community service. She was ecstatic when she ran into the group of Americans, which included Sergio, and found out that they were from the college that she and Paul were planning to attend.

Wendy and Sergio were immediately at odds with each other. She was out to evangelize the people with the message that Jesus was the answer to every problem, including poverty, starvation, drought, and the AIDS epidemic. He'd thought she was cute, sexy even, but totally ridiculous. As far as Sergio was concerned, European colonists and their Christianity were largely to be blamed for the problems many Africans faced.

They'd butted heads and argued vehemently, although he longed to redirect her passion to his bedroom. Wendy wasn't having it. She was saved and sanctified, and she was saving her virginity for some guy back in New York named Paul Chambers whom she planned to marry as soon as they obtained their parents' approval.

"Lucky guy," Sergio had thought back then. "Jerk," he thought now as he gazed across the field to where Wendy was standing. He too had heard the news about Paul and Constance's engagement, and he knew the news must have struck Wendy like a dagger to her heart.

He longed to go to her and provide her with a shoulder to cry on. From his vantage point, she was coping impressively well.

He shifted his focus as a female, dressed in skintight shorts that stopped above her thighs, blocked his view.

"Hi, Sergio," she greeted him in a sultry voice.

He smiled at her and glanced at the other guys sitting at the table. He was accustomed to good-looking females pushing up on him. The guys nearby watched with envy, while the other females viewed her with disdain. Sergio smiled.

"I'm Kiki Daniels." She placed her right hand in his and let it relax there, providing more of a caress than a handshake. "I'm told that you're the resident expert on Africana Studies, that you're campaigning for Barack Obama, and running for SGA president this year. I'm very interested in working on your campaign."

Kiki leaned forward, but Sergio averted his gaze from her low-cut blouse. His eyes met hers and he appeared unaffected by her seductive body language and sultry tone of voice. Kiki was new to the campus. She would soon learn the reasons for Sergio's reputation as an undercover lover. He connected with women one on one, privately and personally. Normally, he would take a stroll with a girl like Kiki and become more acquainted, laying the foundation for a date. Today, however, he was concerned about Wendy.

"Anyone at this table can tell you about the college's premier Africana Studies program," Sergio replied, extricating his hand. He introduced the others. "I'll be back," he stated and slipped away.

CHAPTER THREE

Showtime.

Constance inhaled dramatically, weary from telling everyone else what to do. She put on the persona of a diva. She wasn't being true to herself, but the image seemed to work for her. She and Paul were probably the most famous students on their college campus. She was happy that she'd latched on to Paul when she met him two summers ago. He'd looked so lonely then, wailing a sorry tune on his saxophone. She had hung back silently in the shadows of the music room and listened. His music had captured the loneliness in her own heart. Eventually, he put down his sax and spun to face the piano he'd been leaning against. That's when she joined him. Together, they had played an old love song.

She smiled at him now as she climbed onto the wooden stage that had been erected for the talent show segment of the college fair. He looked troubled, she thought, and suspected that he might be thinking about Wendy. It didn't make sense for her to worry about that now while she was getting ready to host the show.

She flashed a brilliant smile at her co-host as they met each other center-stage. They kissed each other on the cheek and turned to face the crowd gathered on the playing field.

"Get ready! Get ready! Get ready!" her blond hair, blue-eyed co-host shouted into his microphone.

Call it political correctness or an achievement of balance, she and her co-host Brad reflected the two races that characterized the majority of students on campus.

"Get ready! Get ready! Get ready!" Constance echoed.

The speakers blared out a heavy beat. Performers took their positions near the stage.

"It's Showtime. Boom. Na na na na. Na na na, nana, nana."

Constance and Brad shouted into the microphone, as they shook their bodies to the rhythm of the music and danced across the stage. They caught the crowd's attention. People moved away from the display tables and positioned themselves where they could watch the show.

"Get ready! Get ready! Get ready!" Constance shouted, shaking her chest and hips, while jerking her bent arms forward in front of her.

"Get ready! Get ready! Get ready!" Brad echoed, imitating her movements.

The music played and they danced some more. As they bumped hips, the crowd let out a roar.

"Holler back, if you're ready," Brad cried.

"Holler!" the crowd replied.

"Holler back, if you're ready," Constance echoed.

Again the crowd roared, "Holler!"

"Bring Da Noise."

Constance and Brad dragged out the sound of their final three words as they left the stage.

A Hip Hop dance troupe called Da Noise took their place with the first performance. A couple dancing to a song that was on top of the Pop charts followed them. After that came folk dancers of various cultures dressed in modest traditional clothing. Then came the modern dancers dressed in skimpy outfits exposing their torso and thighs.

In between each performance, Constance and Brad returned to the stage to hype up the audience and taunt the judges.

All the modern dancers moved seductively. Dancers in tight clothing, shaking and rotating their hips, some even dropping suggestively to the floor. The crowd went wild.

Wendy's group mounted the steps.

Donna felt intimidated. She was certain that, after all the flexing and winding of the preceding dancers, their liturgical dance group would be booed right off the stage. She looked out into the audience and noticed that as they came into view, onlookers seemed to turn their attention elsewhere. She knew that they were visually less appealing than the group that preceded them because their bodies were modestly clothed in a leotard and long skirt.

The heavy reggae beat of the song they were dancing to kicked in, taking the crowd by surprise.

"With long life, you satisfy me, you satisfy me, with long life... I will praise you forever..."

The crowd joined in, singing the simple lyrics and swaying to the rhythm of the hit song by Israel and New Breed. Wendy's group danced, but the emphasis of their movement was on their arms and hands rather than on their hips. They waved a sheer scarf heavenward, adding grace and elegance to their motions.

Donna was surprised when the crowd erupted in applause and shouted approval at the end of their performance.

"They call themselves Faith Works," Brad announced, as he and Constance returned to the stage.

"Yeah! And they took us to church on that one," Constance observed, stomping her feet, jerking her body, and waving her right hand in the air.

Brad pretended to fan her to cool her down. "Amen, Sis. Constance," he joked.

"I... I... I feel the power of the Holy Ghost," Constance declared dramatically.

The crowd laughed.

Paul watched from behind the stage with a serious expression on his face. He understood that Constance and Brad's joking was a necessary part of the entertainment, but he disapproved of their irreverence. Especially Constance, she should know by now how he felt about that. He expected her to know better than to make a mockery of what Christians like him considered serious praise.

The music stopped for a moment. Brad cleared his throat. "We now pause for a public service announcement." The audience listened expectantly.

"Don't forget to register to vote!" Brad and Constance yelled into their microphones.

Instantly, the music came back on and the crowd grew noisy again.

"Get ready, ya'll, for the final segment of the talent show," Brad announced. "The next set of performers will sing solo."

"How low will they go?" Constance asked.

"So low that you can't hear them."

"Ha, ha."

Their corny old joke produced more sneers and jeers than laughter among the audience.

"The winner will get a chance to perform live on stage with none other than our very own, Stellar and Dove Award winning, Best New Artist, my fiancé Paul Chambers."

Constance paused as the audience cheered. She held up her left hand so that her diamond engagement ring would glisten in the sunlight.

Wendy felt a sense of panic rise within her. She couldn't take much more of this. She wanted to run far, far away, so she wouldn't have to hear Constance boasting about being engaged to her one and only true love. Silently, Wendy prayed and mentally reviewed Scripture to help her withstand the emotional turmoil that was brewing within.

"I can do all things through Christ who strengthens me." She mentally replayed that verse from Philippians 4:13 over and over again as she prepared herself to return to the stage. This time she'd face the crowd alone, without the company of the other dancers.

Wendy's voice was powerful, and as she sang, she belted out a range of notes that took the audience on a musical journey from a hollow place inside her to a high-pitched hope that transcended their grasp.

Paul felt so proud of her, he longed to run to her and wrap her in his arms. He had been praying that she could do this. He knew that her faith in God would bolster her to sacrifice her own feelings for the mission of spreading the gospel. Wendy sang about Jesus, just like she and he used to do in the talent shows they entered and won when they were in high school. He was certain she would win this time.

She did.

The audience went wild when Paul came on stage. They were familiar with his music. He performed many of his songs live on campus before they were recorded and aired on the radio. Much of the audience didn't listen to the type of Jesus music Paul sang, but they got caught up in the excitement of having a small time celebrity on campus.

"Thank you," Paul shouted into the microphone. "Thank you." He waved at the audience before pointing to a group of girls standing near the stage.

They squealed.

Sergio shook his head as he noticed that the group included some of the women from the African and American Students Union table. Based on how they had sneered at Wendy and her prayer group earlier, he expected them to appear aloof. He had a good excuse for moving forward, near the front of the stage. He was there to support his friend Wendy.

"I thought you weren't into this kind of music," he shouted above the noise to the girl closest to him.

She giggled. "I don't care if Paul Chambers is singing about Jesus or Jungle Juice. He sounds good. Hmm mm. The brother got some pipes on him."

"Whatever."

Sergio spotted Wendy standing in the background with the other soloists while Paul performed his first number. Then his gaze shifted critically to focus on Paul. To him, Paul looked tall and skinny. Paul was physically fit, but he lacked the well-defined muscles that Sergio flexed visibly at his slightest movement. Sergio was a biker and he spent hours working out in the gym. His magnetism stemmed from his good looks, academic brilliance and laid back personality. Paul, on the other hand, sought attention through his music and attracted the ladies because of his newfound fame.

At that moment, Sergio felt no respect for him. He knew Wendy had loved Paul before all this. The fact that Paul snubbed Wendy for a relationship with Constance, the daughter of a media mogul, made Paul seem like an opportunist. Constance managed Paul's career, and it was her connections that had launched him to stardom.

Constance joked with Brad offstage as she watched her fiancé perform. She was proud of him, and pleased with herself for recognizing talent and uncovering it for the world to hear his music. When she'd first made the suggestion to Paul, he expressed no interest in a music career. In fact, he was dead-set against it. As she got to know him better and realized that what motivated him was a heartfelt desire to tell the world about Jesus, she managed to convince him that a music career was one way he could effectively do that.

She glanced over at Wendy, weary that there wasn't a better female vocalist on campus. She would rather have had anyone else sing with Paul. She knew Wendy was Paul's high school sweetheart and that they had been childhood friends. Paul seemed to have gotten over her to the extent that he had spent little or no time with her during the past four semesters. But when they sang something troubling happened that Constance couldn't quite explain.

Constance's eyes followed Paul as he moved around on the stage. She wished he had opened his performance by declaring his love for her. That would have warned Wendy and everyone else to back off because he loved her. Instead, he hadn't acknowledged her in any special way.

Wendy closed her eyes and said a final silent prayer as she prepared herself to face Paul on stage.

"I can't do this," she thought. "I can't face Paul again. Not after the way he looked at me earlier, making me feel like he still loved me, like he cared and wanted to be with me. Only to find out that Constance was wearing his ring…"

She gasped at the thought. She wanted to curl up on the floor somewhere and weep. At the same time, she knew she couldn't pass up this opportunity. Each time she and Paul lifted their voices together to praise God, they forgot about themselves and the worship experience took over, bringing members of their audience to tears. For many, it was a life changing experience that caused them to approach Paul and Wendy to find out more about forming their own relationship with the Lord Jesus.

"I can do all things through Christ who strengthens me," Wendy whispered fiercely and took a step forward.

Paul turned to face her and as she approached, he belted out one of Israel and New Breed's songs, "Where would I be if not for your grace?"

Wendy inhaled deeply and exhaled her response, "Where would I be if not for your grace?"

They sang a medley of songs that were popular on the gospel and contemporary Christian music charts. The object of their adoration was the Lord, but a powerful chemistry churned between them that made their audience wonder if they shared more than a microphone.

As Sergio watched, he was baffled by the strength he saw in Wendy. He remembered that he'd never seen her perform this well. Paul and Wendy connected in such an intimate way that Sergio questioned whether they had been lovers, in spite of Wendy's insistence during their prior conversations that she and Paul had been saving themselves for marriage to each other. A lover's passion was the only emotion that Sergio knew that could consume two people in such oneness.

Constance couldn't wait for the performance to end. She understood the spiritual uplifting that took place during praise and worship. In church, she often saw people act like they lost their mind, shouting, "Hallelujah!" at the top of their lungs when they got caught up in the Holy Spirit. Personally, she never experience that loss of control, but she observed it often enough. The sight of Wendy and Paul singing together alarmed her. Sure, they appeared to be consumed by the Holy Spirit, but their togetherness bothered her—the oneness of their experience. Had they been singing secular love songs, there would be no denying that they appeared to be lovers.

"Never could have made it without you." Paul's voice resonated with emotion, as he sang Marvin Sapp's hit song.

Again, Constance wanted to stop the show. The song was about salvation and the Lord Jesus, but the message that Paul could not have made it without Wendy was implied.

"I would have lost it all, but now I see how you were there for me." Wendy held the microphone in her left hand and raised her right hand heavenward as she sang.

Together they sang praise to the Lord God.

Paul focused on Wendy and took a step toward her with each phrase.

Wendy didn't budge. Her peripheral vision revealed that Paul was getting closer. Turning to walk toward him would seem like a natural response, but Wendy couldn't do it. She couldn't face him as they sang this closing number with unchecked emotion.

They sang, "When I look back over all you brought me through, I can see that you were the one that I held on to."

Paul grasped Wendy's hand.

Wendy's eyes filled up and overflowed with tears.

Constance wanted to charge onto the stage and separate them.

One of her sorority sisters pulled her aside and commented. "That looks like more than the Holy Spirit flowing between Wendy and your future husband."

Constance flashed her a confident smile, but she was furious with Paul.

Wendy didn't pull her hand away. It would have caused too much of a scene. But she still refused to look at Paul.

Paul caressed her hand with his thumb, a silent way of saying he was sorry. The lyrics of Marvin Sapp's hit song had a dual meaning for him. Yes, he praised God for saving his soul, but he also felt God had used Wendy to bolster his faith. Through the self-consciousness of their adolescent years, they were together, and together, they boldly shared their faith. Every year, when they were in high school, they entered the talent show together and won. Each time they sang about Jesus, and sometimes Paul would back Wendy up by playing music on the piano, guitar, or saxophone. As a teenager, Paul found it much easier to stand up for Jesus because with Wendy by his side, he never had to stand alone.

The song ended and Paul continued to hold Wendy's hand as they took a bow.

Wendy wished he would let her go. She wanted to run away, but if she tried to pull her hand from his and he resisted, she would draw even more attention to herself.

The moment the song ended, Constance charged forward. As Paul and Wendy straightened from their bow, she grabbed their hands and pulled them apart. "Give it up for my fiancé," she shouted into the microphone. She turned her back toward Wendy, placed her hands on both sides of Paul's cheeks and kissed him.

Wendy ambled off stage, but the moment she reached the bottom of the steps, she walked briskly away from the crowd.

CHAPTER FOUR

Sergio weaved his way through the crowd and followed Wendy down the pathway that led away from the field, past the classrooms, to the dorms.

"Come home with me," he suggested, as he caught up with her and began walking by her side.

She turned to face him, her eyes glistening with tears. A spoken word would cause the tears to fall. She kept walking.

"Everyone will be heading back to the dorms in a little while," Sergio explained. "You can have my place to yourself. I'll even leave you alone there, if you want me to." He didn't want to leave her alone there. He wanted to hold her in his arms and ease her pain. Yet, all that mattered to him at that moment was her feelings. He would do anything to make her feel better.

Was that love? Sergio thought to himself as Wendy changed direction and started walking with him toward the campus gates. People accused him of constantly breaking hearts. Woman after woman threw herself his way. He enjoyed each one, for a time, before closing the door and moving on. He felt it was their fault if they took him so seriously as to fall in love with him.

It seemed like he could never get Wendy to take him seriously enough. He felt so protective of her that at that moment he wanted to punch Paul in the face. He thought Paul was either blind or stupid for rejecting the love Wendy so freely and generously reserved exclusively for him.

Sergio lived in an apartment complex midway between the downtown business district and the vast college campus. That residential area attracted many of the older college students and graduate students who desired independent living situations away from the limitations of dorm life. Wendy remembered that this was the same neighborhood where she and Paul had imagined they would get an apartment to live in as a married couple while they were completing their college education.

As Sergio unlocked the door to his apartment, Wendy inhaled the faint aroma of cooked food. She breathed deeply.

Sergio smiled. "Are you hungry? I made callaloo and saltfish with fried dumplings for breakfast this morning. There is some leftover in the kitchen."

Wendy headed for the kitchen. "Really now?" She called out over her shoulder. "What do you know about callaloo? I bet you made collard greens."

Sergio met her at the stove and opened a pan to display a dark green cooked vegetable seasoned with chunks of tomato and codfish. "I know that callaloo is a vegetable that people grow in Jamaica that cooks up a lot like collard greens. The question is, can you tell the difference?" He raised a forkful to her mouth.

"Yum." Wendy licked her lips as she savored the food. She took the fork from his hand and fed herself another mouthful. She nodded. "This is good." She stepped over to the sink and quickly washed her hands with dishwashing liquid, before opening the cupboard to find a plate. She shared three golden brown fried dumplings onto the plate with a heap of the vegetable dish.

Sergio watched her with a grin on his face. He was glad that she was making herself at home. In the two years he'd known her, she rarely visited his place. He also felt relieved that instead of the outburst of crying he was expecting the moment they were alone, Wendy was consumed by her enjoyment of the food he'd cooked.

"Care to sit down?" He motioned toward some stools at a tall, circular dining table.

Wendy looked beyond the dining table, over the half-wall, to the sofa in the living room.

"Go ahead," Sergio invited. "I'll get us a drink."

Wendy sat on the black leather sofa and pulled a lever that caused the seat to adjust, allowing her to extend her legs out in front of her.

Sergio brought her a glass of grapefruit soda on ice.

Wendy gulped down the cold drink. "You couldn't have done better if you were expecting me over for a date."

Sergio raised and lowered his eyebrows. "Maybe I was."

"Stop playing. Knowing you, you have a date planned for this evening, but it sure wasn't with me. Who is the lucky woman?"

He smiled confidently and sat in a chair adjacent to hers.

Wendy stared directly into his eyes as she waited for his answer.

"LaTanya Monroe. Do you know her?"

Wendy squinted her eyes at him. "Yeah. She is a transfer student. Went to college in Connecticut. Grew up in Jamaica."

He nodded. "That's the one."

"She is so preppy. I wouldn't have thought you were her type."

Sergio lifted the long strands of his dreadlocks and dropped them over his shoulders. "I'm every woman's type. Can I help it if women find me irresistible?"

Wendy cleared her throat. "Intolerable," she said, correcting him, laughing as she tossed one of his red, green and gold cushions at him. "Clearly, she hasn't yet learned about your reputation."

He caught it and leaned forward, holding it between his legs. "Ever faithful. Ever true."

"You are… as a brother, or a cousin, but not as a boyfriend."

"Are you sure about that now?" Sergio rose from his seat and sat beside her. "You don't need to rely on second hand information to find out."

Wendy straightened the chair and got up. "Okay. Thanks for the meal. That's my cue to leave."

Sergio blocked her path and took the plate from her hands. "Don't leave. You know I respect your boundaries, but you can't blame a guy for trying. You're a beautiful woman, Wendy, and pretty irresistible yourself."

"Apparently, Paul doesn't think so."

Sergio placed the dirty dishes in the sink and ran some water over them. "Paul is a First Class Idiot," he said as he turned off the tap and faced her.

"He is supposed to be my fiancé," Wendy said pouting.

"Why? Constance is a better candidate for Mrs. First Class Idiot."

Wendy laughed but her eyes filled up with tears again.

"Will you stop wasting your life on that guy?" Sergio demanded, hugging her.

The tears streamed down her face. "You don't know him like I do," Wendy explained, sniffling. "I don't know what's going on, but he still loves me. We promised we would save ourselves for each other. He is supposed to marry me. Nobody else."

Sergio resisted the urge to say, "Yeah, yeah." He had heard it all before. Instead, he stroked her hair and let her cry.

"Did you know that we've known each other all our lives?" Wendy asked.

Sergio nodded, as if she hadn't told him that many times before.

"We grew up in church together. Paul has always been my best friend. He looks out for me. We take care of each other."

Sergio thought to himself, "Maybe in the past, but not so in the last two years." Yet, he said nothing because saying so would only make her cry harder.

"When we were sixteen, we promised to save ourselves for each other."

"What makes you think that Paul is still honoring that promise?"

"I know him. Paul always keeps his word."

"Wendy, Paul is engaged to marry someone else."

She started bawling and pulled herself away from Sergio. "I don't believe it. This is like a nightmare I can't wake up from. Paul wouldn't do that to me. He wouldn't do that. He wouldn't."

"He did," Sergio wanted to say, but that would make her hurt more. Wendy curled up on the sofa sobbing.

Sergio stooped down in front of her. He wanted to hurt Paul for causing her so much pain. "Wendy."

Tears streamed down her face, as she sobbed, but she refused to look at him.

Sergio mentally searched for the right words to say. "Come on now, Wendy. Nobody is worth losing your sanity for. You are too smart, and your future is too bright. Remember, you're sailing through college on a full scholarship."

"I can't go back there. I can't go through the semester seeing Paul and Constance together like they were today." She sat up and shook her head. "I can't do it. I can't do it. I can't." She was sobbing uncontrollably, tears streaming down her face.

"You can and you will," Sergio insisted.

Wendy shook her head. "You don't know how I feel. It's like my heart is hurting. I would rather die."

Now, Sergio was worried. He sat on the sofa beside her, draped his arm around her shoulder, and pulled her against him. He opened his mouth to speak, and closed it again.

"Why doesn't he love me?" Wendy asked, softly. "Why doesn't he want me anymore?"

"Because he's a fool." Sergio wrapped both arms around her and squeezed her tightly for a moment. He reached for one of his red, green, and gold cushions and placed it on his lap. Then, he guided Wendy to rest her head against it. "If Paul is too blind to see how much you love him, after all you say you've been through together, he doesn't deserve you."

"But I still love him," she whined.

"Okay." Sergio paused and then added, "Love conquers all."

Wendy liked that idea: love conquers all. Combined with her belief that God is love, it gave her comfort as she rested her head in Sergio's lap. Amid the sniffles, she yawned.

"Love conquers all," she repeated. "The Bible says, 'Love never fails.'"

"Okay. Same thing," Sergio agreed.

"You know what?" she asked sleepily, yawning again.

"What?" Sergio asked, stroking her hair.

"God is love."

Those were the last words Wendy spoke before she fell asleep.

Sergio listened as her sobs lessened and were replaced by deep breathing. He knew her faith was so strong that she had to be okay. He would stay with her tonight. He was sure he could sweet talk LaTanya into going on a date with him again some other time. For now, not even the thought of an intimate night with a sexy, liberal transfer student could get him to leave Wendy's side.

CHAPTER FIVE

Paul couldn't put the task off any longer. It was a small world and news traveled fast. If he didn't face his mother now, he was sure someone else would inform her that he was engaged to marry Constance. He knew he had to tell her in person.

His cell phone rang just as he was driving away from the college campus.

"What's up, Constance?" he asked speaking into the phone's headset.

"I miss you already. Are you sure you don't want me to come with you?"

"I'm sure. I haven't been home all summer. I need to face Ma alone after staying away for so long."

"It's not like you didn't see her. She came out to your show twice while we were on tour."

"Yes, and she made it clear that she wasn't pleased that I hadn't come home."

"Did you remember to bring the jewelry I bought her?"

"Got it."

"I hope she likes the necklace and earrings."

"She will." He paused and then said, "I'll let you know."

Constance longed to say that she hoped Paul's mother liked her, but she also didn't want him to know how insecure she felt about their relationship at that moment. Instead she said, "Drive safely. Call me when you get there."

"I will."

The drive from suburban New Jersey into New York City did little to relax Paul. As traffic increased, so did the tension he felt as he got closer to home. His engagement was supposed to be good news. Yet, instead of feeling excited, he bristled himself for a confrontation with his mother.

Paul squeezed into a parking spot on the block where his mother lived. Mid-day Saturday on a warm September morning brought the neighbors out. As he crossed the street and headed for the adjoining brick row houses where he had grown up, he spotted his mother who was stooped over, vacuuming the inside of her car. The noise of the hand-held vacuum drowned out his footsteps. A few of the neighbors saw him approaching, but Paul placed an index finger against his lips to urge them to be quiet.

He sneaked up behind his mother, but she turned around just as he was about to tap her on the shoulder.

She screamed.

He hugged her.

A moment later, after she recovered from being startled by his presence, she said, "Paul Patrick Chambers. What are you doing here? Don't tell me that you dropped out of school because you now think you're a superstar." She wagged her finger at him as she spoke.

"Ma, you know me better than that."

"Do I? These days I have to wonder."

Her comment unnerved Paul, but he didn't have a chance to respond to it as the neighbors came over to greet him. Many had known him since he was a little boy and took personal pride in the fact that he had not only gone off to college, but he had also successfully launched a music career. People came out with cameras to take pictures with him and to ask for his autograph.

A whole hour passed before he and his mother finally went inside.

Paul went straight to the bathroom to wash his hands. His next step would be to raid the refrigerator.

"I know you're hungry," his mother said, anticipating his needs. "Shall I whip you up some breakfast?"

"Got any leftover dinner?" Paul asked opening the refrigerator. He could make himself bacon and eggs anytime, but his mother's home cooked dinner was something he hadn't eaten in a long time.

"Look on the second shelf. There is some chicken, and macaroni and cheese, cold slaw and potato salad."

"Mm Good," Paul declared, as he reached for the containers.

"God knew why I was cooking so much food last night. I wasn't expecting company. I just made enough so I wouldn't have to cook for the rest of the weekend."

"Mother's intuition. Deep down inside, you knew I was coming."

"Maybe."

Madge watched her son move around the kitchen. He piled the food up on a plate and stuck it in the microwave. She had a lot to say to him. She needed to scold him, but for now, she would just let him enjoy his meal. As Paul walked over to the dining table, he lifted a chicken leg from his plate and took a bite. "Mm. This is good. I miss your cooking, Ma."

"Obviously not enough to bring yourself around here more often," Madge uttered, under her breath.

Paul heard her clearly, and he knew he had a tongue-lashing coming, but for now, he focused on devouring the food.

Madge rose from the table and poured two glasses of fruit punch. Paul gulped his down and sat back in the chair.

"So, to what do I owe the pleasure of this surprise visit?" she asked him.

Paul smiled at her. "I didn't know I needed a special reason to come home."

"You act like it. Running around the world with that little rich princess girlfriend of yours, staying in expensive hotels and acting like you're too good to come near the Bronx."

Paul took a deep breath and exhaled. "Mommy, I'm sorry I haven't been home all summer."

"Oh, I'm Mommy now. And this is still home? You could have fooled me, you and your uppity girlfriend."

Paul laughed awkwardly. "Ma, about Constance..."

"That's her name. Little Ms. Constance Channing. That diva done filled your head up so much that you forgot where you come from."

The distaste Madge expressed for Constance stumped Paul. She had told him many times that she wouldn't accept anybody else for him but Wendy. Yet, he thought the fact that he and Wendy hadn't gotten back together over the last two years would have softened her attitude.

Paul mentally searched for the words. He smiled at his mother and continued speaking, "Constance and I..."

"Let me guess. Constance and you broke up." Madge incorrectly filled in the rest of her son's sentence. "Thank you, Jesus. Please tell me that's why you're here this weekend? I know dating someone on your college campus is like dating someone who lives on your block. You keep seeing them, whether you want to or not. So, you came here this weekend to get away from her. Right?"

Paul felt dumbfounded. He wondered if she already knew about the engagement and was purposely making it hard for him to tell her, or did she really dislike Constance that much.

He inhaled deeply and exhaled his confession, "Ma, Constance and I are engaged."

Madge wrinkled her brows at him and leaned her head back. "What kind of nonsense are you telling me? I sent you away to college to gain an education, not to lose your mind."

Paul closed his eyes for a moment, wishing he could reopen them to a scenario in which his mother was not so upset.

Madge stood up and touched Paul's forehead with the palm of her hand to test his temperature. "Are you feeling alright?"

Paul chuckled. "Yes, Ma. I'm fine."

"I don't think so, Paul. My son spent seventeen years of his life starry-eyed over Wendy Tapper Douglas." Madge alternated between resting her hands on her hips and waving them about, gesticulating as she spoke. She referred to Paul in the third person, as though she was talking to someone else, and Paul wasn't even there. "'There is no other girl for me,' he used to say. Wendy was the only person he would ever want to marry whether he was seventeen or seventy. 'I want to marry her now, Ma,' he told me when he was in his senior year of high school." Then, she stopped pacing and faced Paul. "You used to say, God's plan for your life and Wendy's was for you to get married during the summer before you started college, and you would live together while you were in college, and migrate to Africa to work as missionaries after you earned your degree. What happened to that plan, Paul?"

Paul sat before her with his shoulders slumped. He listened carefully to his mother's words and watched her as she paced the room.

"Did God change his mind or did you?" she added.

That was a question Paul could not answer. Everything his mother said was true. He loved Wendy. He wanted to marry Wendy. Wendy was the only girl for him. Never had he ever imagined that he would date anyone else much less commit himself to marry another woman. But it was Wendy who changed everything between them when she went off to Africa without him. If she hadn't met her daddy for the first time that year, she would never have been able to afford to take that trip. Her daddy's money had given her the power to do things that Paul couldn't afford to do. Paul still fumed that he hadn't had the money to go with her. She should have waited for him. Africa was their dream. God's plan for their lives. Something they were supposed to experience together. Wendy didn't think twice about how much she hurt him when she went off on her own.

When Paul didn't answer, his mother continued. "I'll tell you what happened." She nodded and walked toward him. "You let jealousy and anger harden your heart."

Paul knitted his brows, hurt by his mother's assessment of him. He stood up and faced her eye to eye. "What do you mean, Ma?"

Madge replied in a much gentler voice. "It seems like it was just yesterday when you stood here before me wearing the Yankees jersey and baseball cap that Wendy gave you. You were saying goodbye. Leaving for college before Wendy got back from her trip to Africa because she hurt your feelings and you didn't want to sit around here crying about it anymore."

Paul turned away from her.

"Isn't that the truth, Paul? How many of your decisions since then have been made because you've been running away from your true feelings for Wendy?"

His mother's words hit home and seemed to melt away the ice that had frozen over his heart. He blinked as his eyes burned with unshed tears. He shook his head impatiently. That summer before he left for college, he had promised himself that he would never again shed a tear over Wendy. Yes, he loved her with a sincere, forever kind of love, but he had promised himself that he would not give her a chance to break his heart again.

He took a deep breath and turned to face his mother. "Ma, I didn't come here to talk about Wendy. You know she goes by her father's last name now, Douglas. Anyway, I came to tell you about Constance."

Madge sighed heavily. She recognized the hardheadedness in his behavior and swayed between blaming herself and his deceased father. "Okay, Son." She sat down in the sofa in the living room. "Tell me about Constance."

Paul walked closer to her, but he leaned against the doorway between the living and dining rooms, instead of sitting down.

"Ma, you'll like Constance if you take the time to get to know her. She is a lot like me. She is passionate about music. She tries to help her neighbors, globally and at home. She encourages me to fulfill my dreams and be the best that I can be." He paused.

Madge stared at him, willing herself to hold her tongue. She and Paul had always had a close relationship. In the relationship between them as single mother and her only child, Paul played the role of a friend, and man of the house, as well as her son.

"I owe her for my music career, Mom."

"I don't think you should give her credit for your God given talents."

"Ma, it takes more than a good voice and musical talent to launch a career in the music industry. Thanks to Constance and her connections, I've taken my music straight to the top."

"Praise the Lord, Son. Give God the praise."

"I do, Ma. You know I do. You always say that God puts people in our lives for a reason. God used Constance to fill a void in my life."

"A void that was previously filled by Wendy."

"Ma!"

"Can you deny that, Paul? All your life, except for the past two years, you've lived in this house. You never complained about feelings of emptiness. Your life revolved around God, music, and Wendy. Do you mind telling me when you first noticed this void?"

Paul looked down at his sneakers.

His mother waited a moment, and then continued. "Wendy loves you, Paul. I've been praying that you'd finally forgive her for going off to Africa without you…"

"I forgave her a long time ago," Paul interrupted her.

"Did you really? So why haven't you and her remained friends?"

"We are friends, Ma. Wendy and I talk when we see each other on campus. She is just not my girlfriend anymore. She chose not to be. Constance is the woman I want to marry."

"Paul, you may think you're a grown man, but you're still under twenty-one."

Paul shrugged. "We're not getting married now. Constance is graduating next summer, but we plan to wait another year, until after I finish my degree."

Madge tried to remain calm as she listened, but she felt like she wanted to throttle him. Perhaps a good shake would remind him of all the years he'd spent trying to convince her that she should allow him to marry Wendy the summer after they finished high school. "You've known Wendy all your life. What is it about Constance that would make her replace Wendy as the girl you want to marry?"

"She loves music. You already know that she writes songs. We share a strong chemistry when we're working on our music together. She inspired me to write the song that won both the Stellar and the Dove award. I couldn't have done that without her. I owe her for the success of my music career."

"You don't owe her your life," Madge croaked, her voice raspy with concern.

Paul heard her clearly.

"What makes you think I feel that way, Ma?"

"Marriage is a lifetime commitment, Paul. Is Constance the only woman you want to spend the rest of your life with?"

"Constance loves me and is devoted to me in a way that Wendy was not."

Madge felt both surprised and enlightened by that remark. "What makes you think so?"

"Constance let's me lead. When Wendy left for Africa, she showed me that she didn't care much for the direction I wanted us to go."

Madge nodded. She understood. She also realized that arguing with Paul now would not make him understand. She had to pray about this first. With the insight Paul had just given her, she would continue to present her son, along with Constance and Wendy, to the Lord.

Paul called his Pastor that evening. Reverend Walker had served as a father figure in Paul's life while he was growing up. The Pastor and his wife had children of their own, but they genuinely cared for the church-children like extensions of their own family. Paul and Wendy were particularly dear to the Pastor's heart because they had publicly championed the cause of abstinence until marriage in a way that not even the Pastor's biological children had.

"Hello."

Paul felt a mixture of excitement and regret when he heard the reverend's deep voice on the end of the line. "Good evening, Reverend Walker. It's Paul Chambers."

"Paul Chambers! How are you, Son?"

"Good. How are you, First Lady Valerie and the rest of the family?"

"Everybody is doing well, praise the Lord! Where are you? I hope you finally came home for a visit."

The Reverend's voice was filled with more warmth than criticism, yet Paul felt guilty.

"Yes, I'm finally home, Sir. Has my mother been complaining?"

"No. She's too proud of you. We all are. She's just a little concerned that you might be losing touch. We've seen that happen time and again when our children go off to college. And you're facing the added demands of your music career. How are you managing?"

"God is good. I spent the summer touring and finally made it to Africa."

"I heard. Wendy was here working with the children in Vacation Bible School the week you were in Africa. She incorporated your experience into the lesson she was teaching, daring the kids to believe that God would do great things in their lives when they put their trust in him."

This was news to Paul. He had assumed that Wendy had spent her summer lounging on the beach on her father's property in Jamaica. The information the reverend just shared reminded him of one of the things he loved about her. Wendy devoted much of her time to working for the Lord. Even as children, they had enjoyed being active in the church. They had looked forward to spending a lifetime together doing God's work.

Paul sighed. Each time he felt he'd gained control of his emotions, someone mentioned Wendy's name and unsettled feelings deep within him.

"Have you seen Wendy since the semester started?" Reverend Walker asked.

"Oh yeah. We have the same major, so we run into each other pretty often."

"Good. My wife and I are believing that this is the year you'll get back together."

"Excuse me?"

"You and Wendy. I know it seemed like I was giving you a hard time when you insisted that you wanted to marry Wendy right after high school, and I refused to perform the ceremony without your parents' permission."

"That was the right thing to do, Reverend. I can see that now."

"Oh. Praise the Lord! I want you to know, Paul, that the next time you and Wendy decide that you're ready to get married, it would be my honor and privilege to perform the ceremony."

Paul squirmed in his seat. Two years ago, he'd longed for his pastor's approval. Now, it only complicated matters, making it harder to tell him that he wanted to marry someone else.

"Did you hear that my Priscilla married Reggie?"

"About a year ago, right? Mom told me. She said both you and Lady Valerie cried at the wedding."

"Hey, now." Reverend Walker laughed. "It's not every day that a father hands his baby girl over to her husband. It's a blessing, but it's hard to give away your daughter."

"I can't imagine what that feels like, but I know Reggie. I think he'll take good care of her."

"I think so too. Keep them in your prayers. They're about to have a baby."

"Congratulations, Pastor! Or should I say, 'Grandpa.'"

"I like the sound of that. Praise the Lord."

They chuckled.

"Will we see you at church tomorrow?" Reverend Walker asked.

"Yes. Pastor, I'd like to surprise everyone."

"Okay. Do you mind if I tell my wife that we spoke?"

"No. Go ahead." Paul didn't want his newfound celebrity status to become a distraction if people were informed in advance that he was coming. He felt Reverend Walker understood that.

"I'll see you in the morning."

"Goodnight, Pastor."

"Goodnight."

Paul and his mother went to earliest service together the next morning. Everything from the big white church to the content of the sermon, reminded Paul of Wendy. Their mothers had brought them there as babies, and together they had grown up there with a love for the Lord that made them stand out among their peers.

Paul and his mother entered the sanctuary before the service began. Members of the choir standing near the door thronged Paul, congratulating him on his music awards. They wanted to know if he had any copies of his CD with him. Everyone wanted an autographed copy. He confessed that he was not prepared, but he promised to come back to do a signing.

At the moment Reverend Walker stood behind the pulpit, he invited Paul to come sing with the choir. Paul climbed onto the choir stand, but his effort to blend in didn't last long before they pulled him forward to sing a solo.

CHAPTER SIX

Paul left home shortly after the Sunday morning service, leaving his mother to inform Reverend Walker and the church folk about his plans to marry Constance. Paul expected that the reverend's reaction would be similar to his mother's. He felt that they were dwelling on the past, focusing on the boy he used to be back when he was determined to marry Wendy. Constance knew and loved the man he had become. He spoke Constance's name out loud to activate the voice command, which speed-dialed her number on his cell phone.

"I was missing you." Constance greeted him cheerily, as she answered the phone.

"Me too," Paul replied.

"I called you earlier, but it went straight to your voicemail."

"I went to church with my mom."

"I should have known. You never miss a service."

"How about you? Did you go to church this morning?"

"Too tired," Constance yawned. "You missed out on all the parties last night. I don't think there was a student in this college town that wasn't out all night."

Instinctively, Paul thought of Wendy. He was certain she wasn't boozing with the crowd, and felt equally assured that she would have attended church that morning.

"Okay," he said, trying not to sound disappointed, but the fact that Constance didn't share his enthusiasm for church, and for spontaneously praising the Lord was a low point in their relationship. "I just wanted to let you know I'm on my way back."

"Cool. Will you pick me up at the sorority house when you get here?"

"What's happening there? Another party?"

"No. Just catching up with the girls. I didn't see most of them all summer. Will you pick me up?"

"Of course."

With that Paul was gone.

Constance stared at the cell phone in her hand, feeling an emotional distance between her and her fiancé. Paul never offered any terms of endearment. No "I love you," no "I miss you. Can't wait to see you, honey." Constance would have loved to hear those words, but she was accustomed to Paul's abruptness. She loved him anyway. Paul was a compassionate human being, and she would rather have a man whose actions demonstrated his love for her, than one who said the words, but didn't show the love.

She snuggled down under the soft, puffy comforter on her bed, trying to identify the point in their relationship when she'd actually begun to feel like she loved him. She remembered the instant connection their love for music sparked between them, as they sang an old love song while Paul played the piano. She might not be able to sing as well as Wendy Tapper, but she could hold her own.

Now, why had her mind drifted to that comparison? She wondered whether Wendy was a real threat to their relationship. She worried about the aura that surrounded Paul and Wendy each time they sang together. There was something powerful, almost tangible, between them that everyone could see. Constance couldn't deny that. Yet, she felt secure in knowing that Paul served the Lord with conviction. Paul and Wendy were the same age. Constance was twenty-one. Yet, Constance felt that Paul would never two-time her with Wendy because he answered to the Lord. She didn't share Paul's religious convictions, but she felt grateful that the accountability he felt to God made him an honest man.

Constance pushed back the covers and got out of bed. She always slept with the air conditioning on high, so she could wrap herself up in the blankets and feel secure. To most people, she appeared to be spoilt and pampered, but there was a lot they didn't know about her. Only Paul had glimpsed the sadness behind the glamour of Constance Channing's designer clothes.

Socially, Constance and Paul were from different worlds, but they shared a common sorrow from having a deceased parent. They bonded over the common experience of knowing that parent only through photographs. For Paul, it was his father's pictures encased in photo albums, occasionally brought to life by his mother's stories. Constance's memories of her mother also consisted of stories told to her by other people, and occasions she viewed in pictures and on videotape.

She knew loneliness. It hurt even more that she hardly ever saw her father, who always made more money available to her than she could spend, but never showed up for even the major milestones in her life. He financed her education at prestigious boarding schools, but he hadn't even bothered to attend her graduation ceremony. Constance could count on being disappointed each time she reached out to her dad. Many of the girls she'd met in boarding school and college envied her because of her father's prominence in the media. Bill Channing was practically a household name. There was only one other person, besides Paul, who knew how estranged Constance was from her father.

The phone rang again. Constance recognized the name of her closest girlfriend on the caller ID.

"Alicia. Hey, girl!"

"Hey, Constance! What are you doing?"

"I was about to take a shower. You? Your house is pretty quiet. Where are Neil and the kids?"

"They are downstairs doing something. I'm having a little me-time, so I'm not really sure."

"And you took the time to call me. I feel so special."

"You are. Don't you forget that, Constance Channing."

"Thank you, Alicia Davis. And you're the best mommy-friend in the whole world."

"Every time you call me your mommy-friend you make me feel old."

"I've been calling you that since we were kids."

Alicia laughed. "I know. Maybe, it's bothering me now because I'm going to turn thirty."

"Golly, woman. Give yourself a break. You just celebrated your twenty-ninth birthday."

"Yeah, but knowing that I'm on the verge of entering another decade is daunting."

"Age is nothing but a number."

"So they say." Alicia paused and then added, "You would feel that way. After all, you went and got yourself engaged to a younger man. A teenager at that. What did your father say?"

"I didn't tell him yet."

"Constance Channing! What are you waiting for?"

"It's not my fault he's never around. Alicia, you know my father. He's never been there when I needed him, so I'm not breaking my neck to get in touch with him."

"Did you at least call him?"

"Yes. I called the same day Paul and I got engaged, right after I talked to you."

"And?"

"His assistant said he was out of the country."

"Did you call his office or his personal cell phone?"

"The number I called was supposed to be his direct line. That's how I reached him the last time we talked."

"When was that?"

"On Father's Day."

"June, July, August, September. You haven't spoken to your father in almost three months."

"That's right. Nothing new there."

"I'm sorry, Connie. I'm praying that the relationship between you and your father will get better."

"Keep praying. It'll take a miracle to make that happen."

"God is able."

"Yeah. Okay."

"Constance, God can bring about a change in your relationship."

"I believe you. I just don't see what difference that will make at this point in my life. I'm twenty-one years old. I can take care of myself now. Where was he all those times I needed him while I was growing up?"

"My guess is that it's been hard for him ever since your mother died."

Constance gasped. "Do you think it's easy for me? That car accident robbed me of both my parents." She started crying. "Mommy died. I can accept that I'll never see her again. But it hurts worse to know that Daddy is right here, but never makes the time to see me."

Alicia had been nine years old when the accident happened. The tragedy had occurred when Constance's mother was driving home from a shopping spree. Alicia's mother was with her. Both women died in the car accident. Constance had been too young to remember what happened. Their fathers were neighbors, and at first the grief brought them closer together. As the years passed, Constance's father buried himself in his work and hired a nanny to nurture Constance. Alicia's father grieved differently. He would scarcely let Alicia leave his side.

Over time, Alicia took on the role of Constance's big sister, and kept in touch with her often, even after Constance's father sent her away to boarding school. Alicia's father remarried and Constance came home to their house on holidays. Constance's father built a multi-billion dollar media corporation, and although he dated many women, he remained married only to his work.

As usual, Alicia tried to think of words that would comfort Constance. "Your father loves you, Constance. He would want to know that you're planning to get married."

"Paul and I aren't getting married right now. I'm graduating at the end of this year, but he still has another year to go after this one. We haven't even started talking about the wedding."

"Did you meet his family?"

"I met his mother."

"That's good. Take your time. Keep a level head. Don't do anything hasty and irreversible."

"Yes, Mommy," Constance joked. "Thanks for always being there for me, Alicia."

"Anytime, girl. I love you."

"I love you, too. Say hi to Neil and kiss the kids."

"Will do."

The closer Paul got to the college campus, the more he struggled to focus his thoughts on Constance instead of Wendy. He remembered how hurt Wendy had looked when she learned of the engagement. He hadn't meant to hurt her and longed to apologize to her. She'd been so strong, he thought, as he recalled how she danced and sang with him on stage. Knowing her the way he did, he knew that must have been hard. Yet, he understood that Jesus was the source of her strength, and through Christ they could do all things.

Was his mother right? He couldn't deny that he still loved Wendy. Of course he did. He loved people. That's what his faith was all about. Love God and love your neighbor was the essence of his beliefs. So, it was only natural that he would always love Wendy, especially because they had grown up so close together. That didn't mean he shouldn't marry Constance. He associated Wendy with the past. Constance consumed his time now, and they faced a promising future of making music together.

He pulled up in front of the renovated old Colonial-style house that served as the meeting place for Constance's sorority. The house was painted in bright colors and had large Greek letters symbolizing the name of the sorority. He dialed Constance's cell phone number to let her know he was parked in front. She didn't answer. He waited a few minutes and tried again.

After the third try, Paul reluctantly got out of the car, climbed the steps and rang the doorbell. The door opened, but he still didn't see anyone, so he stepped inside.

"Surprise!"

Constance stepped forward and wrapped her arms around him.

He returned her kiss.

The other couples standing around the room cheered.

Paul scanned their faces before pausing to read the banner:

"Congratulations on your engagement."

CHAPTER SEVEN

Paul packed up his laptop and paper and headed for the study hall. Perhaps, there he could focus on revising his paper one last time. Sitting alone in his room wasn't working. He'd left the sorority house and dropped off Constance explaining that he had work to do. This paper would determine his grade for an entire course. He hadn't spent enough time working on it over the summer, and his time was about to run out. Again he thought of Wendy. She too enrolled in the independent study course, but knowing her, she would have already finished her paper.

He found a table with students he didn't know, turned on his laptop and sat down. He didn't want to be drawn into a conversation with anyone. Had he and Wendy still been close friends, they would have proofread each other's papers. He was doing it again: engaged to Constance; thinking about Wendy. A guilty feeling gnawed at him because he knew that wasn't right.

"Urban violence and the black community." He read the heading on his paper and willed himself to focus on the topic. When he and Wendy had selected that college for its reputation in Africana Studies, they had expected to focus on a study of Africa. It had taken him by surprise that the professors had made so much comparison between tribal warfare in Africa and black on black violence in the United States.

Wendy and Paul hadn't had to bury a friend during their childhood, but some of their classmates had lost young friends and relatives. Even those students whose lives had been completely sheltered from such loss were shaken by the senseless shooting of four college students at the start of the previous school year. Like many of his peers, Paul saw himself in those victims. They hadn't been involved in any crime; they hadn't gone looking for trouble. Trouble found them just hanging out on a summer day, and three of the four victims had lost their lives.

For the Africana Studies Department, the present school year promised to be uplifting, with all the excitement generated by Senator Barack Obama's bid for the presidency.

During the spring, the entire student body was galvanized around the prospect of electing either the first female or the first African American president of the United States. After Senator Obama secured the Democratic nomination over Senator Hillary Rodham Clinton, some students spent the summer working on his campaign.

By the time the students returned to college for the fall semester, even the most apathetic students were expressing passionate opinions about the upcoming elections. Voter registration tables became a fixture along the campus walkway. As students campaigned for their favorite candidate from the Republican or Democratic Party, support for Senator Obama spread across racial lines. He spoke their language and appeared to be most popular among the college students who admired his intelligence, oratory style, and level of achievement. The support wasn't unanimous though. Some vocal dissenters called him a socialist and argued against his ideas for lifting the American economy out of the recession it was in.

As Paul reread his paper, he wondered how a nation in which African Americans stood on the verge of attaining the highest office, one that history had taught them that they would never occupy, could breed so much intra-racial violence—especially among young black males. The death rate from murder among young men was staggering in some neighborhoods. Senseless crimes where shootings didn't just target the criminal minded, but also claimed innocent lives.

Wendy entered the study hall and scanned the heads in the room, looking for Sergio's signature dreadlocks. He'd asked her to meet him there, but he was nowhere in sight. Instead, she saw Paul. She hadn't expected him to be there. She'd heard about the engagement party for him and Constance over at the sorority house that afternoon. It had taken Sergio's friendship and all the faith in God that she could draw on to stop her from withdrawing from her classes and going home. As her eyes met Paul's, she could feel the tears welling up, but she was determined not to let him, or anyone else who might be watching, see her crying. She spun around to run from the room and found herself blocked by the wall of Sergio's chest.

"Where's the fire?" he asked, placing a hand on her shoulder.

She looked up at him and shook her head.

He noticed her eyes brimming with tears, and looked past her to see Paul staring at them. "Let's take a walk," he said, and kept a protective arm wrapped around her shoulder as they left the room.

They left the building and walked to an area that was more isolated. When he looked at her, there were tears streaming down her face.

"Wendy." Sergio paused, trying to stem the anger he felt toward Paul for breaking her heart. "You can't let him do this to you."

She sobbed.

"He is so not worth it."

"You don't know him."

"I know you, and I know that he's making a big mistake." Sergio wrapped his arms around her and let her cry.

When her sobs subsided, Wendy said, "I can't do this."

"What? Read over my paper," Sergio joked.

"I cannot be here with them."

Sergio knitted his brows at her.

"I can't face Paul and Constance every day, knowing that they are planning to marry each other. I can't do it. I'm going to have to transfer to another college."

"You're made of stronger stuff than that, Wendy. Even if you don't feel like it right now."

"We're in a lot of the same classes. We have the same major. It was hard enough to see him so often when Constance was just his girlfriend. I can't do this knowing that she is going to be his wife."

"This is a test of your faith."

"What?"

"You're always preaching it, Ms. Holy Roller. Scripture Quoter." He placed a hand on his hip and wagged the finger of his other hand as he spoke in a high pitched, feminine voice: "I can do all things through Christ who strengthens me. Oh yeah. Well, it's time to put up or shut up," Sergio concluded resuming his typical masculine stance.

Wendy smiled at him as she thought about what he'd said. He was right, but he didn't have to make fun of her. She punched his arm. "Meanie."

"That's more like it. Get a grip, girl. You're always talking about your Savior. Jesus this. Jesus that. Is Paul Jesus?"

"No."

"Well, you can live without him."

She pouted. "But I don't want to."

"Well, you're going to have to. So get over it already." Sergio pulled out a stack of papers he had rolled up and stuck in the inside pocket of his jacket. "I need you to read this. It's getting late."

She took the papers from him and hit him with them.

"Ouch!" Sergio pretended to be hurt. "That's how you thank me."

"Thank you? Brother, please."

"I tell you, you need to stop thinking about me as your brother. Just give me the chance. I'd make you forget you ever knew anyone named Paul. You'd be too busy screaming my name. Sergio! Sergio!"

"You didn't need to go there," Wendy laughed. "I don't know what

I'm going do with you."
 "You've got to love me."

CHAPTER EIGHT

Wendy approached her class with the resolve to face Paul and not let his presence bother her. Initially, they were scheduled to have two classes together that semester, but she had successfully transferred into another section of one class. She had no choice but to remain in the other class, which was comprised of the ten students who maintained the highest grade point average in the Africana Studies department. They met once a week in their professor's office. Wendy arrived at the first class of the semester a few minutes late. She hadn't wanted to get there too early and risk being alone with Paul before everyone else came into the room.

She sat in the nearest empty seat and listened to the discussion that was already underway.

"That was the most enlightening part of my experience in West Africa. Professor, I know you warned us to be humble and be open to learning from the students and faculty at the University of Ghana, but I still felt confident that as an American, I was going to have the upper hand. What an awakening I had from Africans of every age group who knew so much more than I did! I was far better off once I stopped being condescending and accepted my peers there as equals and esteemed my professors at the University of Ghana as the experts they are."

Professor Robert Abbey grinned, pleased with what he was hearing. When he first moved to the United States from his home in Ghana, he struggled to gain acceptance as an expert in medicine. He didn't take to heart the jokes that were made about him being a bush doctor. Instead, he returned to medical school and obtained American certification in areas he had long studied and worked in while in his native country. Now, he aimed to foster mutual respect between the faculty and students in both countries.

"Any other observations?" he asked the group.

Paul raised his hand. "I was struck by a movement on-campus to reduce the exploitation of women in music videos."

"Yes, I read about that on their web site," Professor Abbey commented. "Perhaps that intrigued you because of your own experience in the music industry."

Paul nodded. "I think it's a good model for what we can do here. We should organize our own music video contest with guidelines indicating that the women in the video must be modestly dressed."

"No rump-shaker videos," another student suggested.

"That will be a switch," someone muttered.

"Yeah—a refreshing change from the typical secular music videos," Wendy said.

"I disagree." The female sitting closest to Wendy objected. Monique reigned as homecoming queen from the previous school year, and many thought she was the prettiest girl on campus. "The typical secular music videos capture life as it is. We live in a sexual society. The women in the videos, rump-shakers and all, represent the people I see around me in the 'hood."

"That may be true," Wendy consented, "but instead of copying what we see around us, a good music video can present society with a goal to aspire to."

"I agree with Wendy," Paul interjected. "I felt empowered by the images I saw in the music videos the college students came up with in Ghana. I may not be a woman, but I'm born of one, and perhaps, I'll have a daughter one day. The best videos from the contest showed women dressed in suits and uniforms. They were directing the action on their job sites. It was inspiring."

"Freedom of choice is the greatest inspiration," Monique countered. "Women have come a long way, yet many still choose to appear scantily dressed in music videos. Some make a good living of it and manipulate the men around them with their sexuality. Modesty has its merits, but I don't think it should be forced on anyone."

The group was thoughtful, but didn't respond immediately.

"Both perspectives are worthy of consideration," Professor Abbey observed. He encouraged free discourse during these sessions, recognizing that sharing different points of view enhanced the learning experience. He lifted one hand as he explained one perspective. "A good music video could set a standard for society to aspire to, as Wendy and Paul argue; however, documenting aspects of today's society is another legitimate function."

"The Bible says that we are to be holy; to present our bodies a living sacrifice to God." Wendy completed her statement, ignoring Monique as she tried to interrupt her by saying, "Here we go again."

"Even God gives us a choice," Paul agreed.

"As advisor to the African and American Students Union, I recommend that you should not restrict the creativity of the contestants, if you organize such a competition," advised Professor Abbey. "Set criteria that won't discriminate against any entrant because of the sexuality or religious viewpoint expressed in the video. The best effort will shine forth as the best, regardless of these factors."

"That's right," Monique quipped. "Freedom of expression. Freedom of choice."

"It's funny how that freedom of expression suddenly stops when I mention the G-word," noted Wendy.

"I don't have a problem with God," Monique retorted, flipping her right index finger up and making a tiny circle with her hand as she spoke. She had mentioned her annoyance with Wendy's holier-than-thou behavior and comments many times before. "It's your limited definition of God that's the problem."

"Excuse me," Wendy and Paul chorused.

Professor Abbey stood up and adjusted his gold metal spectacles. His glasses contrasted sharply with his dark chocolate skin tone. He lifted his copy of the course syllabus and read, "Disagreements will be shared in a respectful manner, allowing each perspective—no matter how unpopular—to be heard. We'll get back to the rules of conduct listed on page three in a few minutes. Let's start on page one of the syllabus."

He asked Monique to read the definition of Africana Studies, which he included on the syllabus.

"Africana Studies is the study of the history, politics, and culture of people of African descent," she read.

"Well done," Professor Abbey thanked Monique before he continued, "Religious beliefs and practices play a pivotal role in the unfolding of the history, politics, and culture of African people throughout the diaspora. I will not censor my students, so I expect each of you to tolerate the airing of different perspectives in this room, regardless of how much those viewpoints differ from your own."

He spent the rest of the class time going over the syllabus and explaining the course requirements for the semester.

Paul caught up with Wendy as she was leaving the building. "That was like old times in there," he stated, when he got close enough for her to hear him. "Like the way we always had each other's back in high school."

She turned to face him, "How can you even think like that when you've gone and hitched yourself up with Constance Channing?"

"We'll always be friends, Wendy." He grasped both of her hands. "The love I have for you will never die."

Wendy felt blindsided by his comments. The declaration of love had come from nowhere, like Cupid's arrow to her heart. She panicked as she envisioned herself breaking down and sobbing in his arms, begging him to break up with Constance and take her back. Instead, she said, "Leave me alone, Paul." She pulled her hands from his and ran away.

CHAPTER NINE

By the time Wendy got to her dorm, she felt silly. How could she have just run away from Paul? She would have to do better. She was made of stronger stuff than that. Her faith was greater than that. She regretted that the person who God had used to bolster her faith was now the same person she needed the greatest faith to face. She still wished she could wake up and find that it was simply a dream, that Paul was really engaged to marry her and not Constance.

She hadn't fallen into a new routine yet for the semester, but there were many things she had to get done. She would be doing an internship that semester. Her initial commitment was just four hours a week, but she was considering adding more hours if she really enjoyed it. The internship didn't pay, so she still wanted to work twenty hours each week at her part-time job. While they were in high school, she and Paul had started earning money through part-time jobs. Some of the money they earned was their spending money to keep back then, but they handed over some of it to their mothers to help pay bills. Such was their life growing up with a single mother who worked a low-income job.

For the past two years though, Wendy's father had offered her a generous allowance. When her father first entered her life during her senior year of high school, Wendy had welcomed and enjoyed spending his money. The unexpected blessing covered her expenses like shopping for the prom and the senior trip. Her biggest ticket item was the round trip to Africa that she charged and then paid for with her daddy's money. After she returned from Africa to find that Paul no longer considered himself her boyfriend, she stopped dipping into her daddy's deep pockets.

She turned on her laptop and logged onto Facebook. The social networking web site was a hub for connecting with people around the world, enabling users to instantly share words and pictures with folks in their directory; folks they casually called friends. While some users maintained hundreds, even thousands, of friends, Wendy had never enjoyed that type of popularity, and she didn't seek it on Facebook.

She found the web site to be a convenient way to connect with her parents, who were both now married to each other and living in Jamaica. Wendy logged on and typed a Scripture for the day in her 'status' box.

"Trust in the Lord with all your heart, and lean not on your own understanding. In all your ways acknowledge Him and He will direct your path," she typed, noting that the verse could be found in the Bible in Proverbs, chapter three, verses five and six.

If Paul had been a friend of hers on Facebook, she knew she could count on him for a positive reply to her posting, but he wasn't her friend. She knew he was on there but she hadn't tried to connect with him. She and Paul used to use their MySpace site to spread the gospel and lift up the name of Jesus. From what she heard, Constance and Paul were using Facebook to promote Paul's music. Even her father had signed up as one of Paul's fans.

She saw a friend request from Jasmine, an old high school and church buddy, but she was reluctant to accept it. She wanted to keep in touch with people from the church she and Paul had grown up in, but she was tired of explaining that she and Paul were not a couple anymore.

"I thought you two would have been married by now," some of the people who'd known them back then would say.

Too often, they concluded by saying, "I know y'all are going to get back together."

Wendy had returned to college optimistic that she and Paul might reunite during that semester, but finding him engaged to Constance shattered that dream.

She noticed that someone had posted, "Amen, Sister Wendy," in response to her Scripture. A thumbnail wedding photo beside the reply revealed that it was her parents.

"Hi, Mommy! What are you doing?" Wendy instant messaged her, so they could have a one-on-one online conversation that everyone else on their Facebook page wouldn't see.

"I just checked in some guests to the hotel and I was enjoying a rare slow moment."

"Cool. How is Dad?"

"Busy. The villas will be opening soon. He's planning a massive media campaign to lure visitors."

"He won't have a problem, I'm sure. It's so beautiful there. Are you loving it?"

"Yes, but I miss seeing you often. And I miss Aunt Pat and Uncle Trev, and Blossom and her family."

"You'll see them soon. Do you and Dad spend a lot of time together?"

"Oh yeah. He will be here in a few minutes to take me to lunch, and we'll be working together for the rest of the afternoon."

"That's nice."

"What are you doing? Are you eating well and taking good care of yourself?"

"Trying."

"How are your classes so far?"

"Good. How is Grandma?"

"She is doing so much better; praise the Lord!"

"Hallelujah! Thank you, Jesus!"

"She is managing a scholarship fund and mentor program for students who can't afford to take dance lessons."

"Go, Grandma! I know she enjoys that. Tell her hi."

"Tell her yourself, missy. Call her when you can."

"I will."

"I love you, Wendy."

"Love you too, Mom. Daddy too."

"Yes."

"Pray for me," Wendy requested.

"Always, in Jesus' name."

They ended the online discussion and Wendy logged off of Facebook. She thought about the romance that had blossomed between her parents during the months after she first met her father. For the first seventeen years of Wendy's life, she knew only her mother, and her father hadn't been there for either one of them. Yet, when God brought him into their lives, she embraced him instantly. It took a lot of prayer and submission to God's word to allow her mother to open her heart to his love. Whenever Wendy considered how unlikely such reconciliation would have been, she praised God. Jesus sacrificed his life so that man's sins could be forgiven, and by trusting in Him, her mother was able to overcome her own hurt and anger and embrace her father in love.

Wendy opened her Bible and turned to first John, chapter four, verses seven and eight.

"Beloved, let us love one another, for love is of God, and everyone who loves is born of God and knows God. He who does not love does not know God, for God is love," she read.

She reflected on the last three words. "God is love."

Wendy flipped the pages back to another section of the Bible where she read the words, "Love never fails." How different was the type of love described in the thirteenth chapter of first Corinthians! It wasn't dependent on the other person's response. It wasn't rooted in conditions like how attractive a lover was, or how well one lover treated another. No. The love described here was permanent; no matter what. That's the type of love she had for Paul.

She prayed for herself and Paul, asking God to guide them, and if it was His will lead them back to each other. She prayed for her family and her peers. By the time she was finished, she felt refreshed and ready to go back out onto the college campus and face her peers, including Paul and Constance.

Each time Marcia felt tempted to worry about Wendy, she prayed instead and had faith that God would watch over, protect, and guide her daughter. She never ceased to pray for Paul, hoping that he and Wendy would get back together and marry each other. As teenagers, Paul and Wendy had tried to convince their parents that an early marriage was God's plan for their lives. Their parents had worked together to get them to postpone the wedding. They hadn't expected a complete break-up, and they knew Wendy was deeply hurt by it. As Marcia saw her husband approaching, she prayed that God would work out a speedy reconciliation between Paul and Wendy.

She stepped out from behind the hotel's front desk and embraced her husband. He kissed her gently on the lips.

"I just finished talking to Wendy on Facebook," Marcia told Devon.

"How's my baby girl?"

"She says she's fine. But I don't know. I know it must be hard for her running into Paul and his fiancée."

"Did you ask her about him?"

"No, I purposely didn't. I didn't want to upset her by talking about him, unless she wanted to."

"That's a sensible approach."

"Thanks."

Devon focused on the woman seated in front of him. He was blessed the day she re-entered his life. From their first meeting, dining over food as they were now, he had respected her for the way she raised Wendy. He hadn't seen her as just his baby-mother back then, and he was grateful to have her as his wife now. She was his best friend. And the way she and their daughter Wendy lived and the praise they constantly gave to God strengthened his own faith.

They sat at a table for two at an outdoor restaurant in their hotel and dined on avocado salad, fried fish, and bammy, flat bread made from cassava.

CHAPTER TEN

Wendy arrived at her internship dressed in a navy blue suit and black heels. Although the internship was a volunteer opportunity, with no salary or stipend attached, she had competed against other students to get it. Her academic counselor told her that only two students from their university were selected, but due to the confidentiality of student records, the counselor could not reveal to Wendy, the other student's name. Wendy looked forward to forging a new friendship. With Paul no longer being her constant companion, Sergio and the girls from the liturgical dance group were her closest friends.

Wendy rode the elevator to the tenth floor of the office building, entered the glass doors, and approached the receptionist's desks.

The receptionist flashed her a smile and hung up the telephone.

"Good afternoon. My name is Wendy Douglas. I'm one of the interns starting today."

"Yes. Welcome. You're right on time. Please have a seat. I'll get someone to escort you to the conference room." The receptionist spoke into the microphone of her headset.

Almost instantly, Wendy noticed a woman walking briskly toward her with a stack of papers.

"Wendy. Welcome. I'm Karlene Bridges, the internship coordinator for the law office. Follow me. We're just about to start the orientation session."

Wendy followed Karlene down another long hallway in the opposite direction from where she had come. As they entered the conference room, Karlene held open the door for her. Inside, a group of young men and women in business suits was seated around a long oblong table.

As Karlene placed the stack of papers on the table, Wendy walked toward the other end of the room and sat in the nearest empty seat. She had tried to be punctual, but the fact that the room was already full of interns made her feel like she was late. The last thing she wanted to do was make a bad impression.

She wanted to check the time, but she felt self-conscious and looked down at the paper in front of her instead. There was an agenda on top. She read it, noticing that the first item was "cocktail hour," a chance for the interns to meet and mingle informally with the attorneys. Her advisor hadn't told her that. That explained why everyone else was so early.

Karlene cleared her throat. "Good afternoon again, everyone. Many of you have already had a chance to meet him; however, I'd like to formally introduce to you Charles Robinson, our director. Mr. Robinson is one of the founders of our organization. He was born and raised right here in this city. He graduated from high school at the top of his class and went on to attain an Ivy League college education, earning both his Bachelor's degree and law degree with honors. He passed the bar exam in New York and New Jersey, and worked in corporate America for eight years before returning to serve his community in the non-profit sector. He has a passion for mentoring young men and women who the media often refer to as inner-city youth, a term Mr. Robinson despises. I present to you, Mr. Charles Robinson."

Mr. Robinson stepped forward and gave Karlene a firm hand-shake. "Thank you."

His small stature surprised Wendy. He seemed much taller on television. He was legendary for representing the underdog and winning difficult cases. Consequently, he commanded the respect of his colleagues. He was the lawyer every guilty criminal wanted to have on their side. Yet, he was a man of integrity.

As he spoke, he highlighted some of the facts that Wendy had researched about him. He had spent years working in the prosecutor's office before crossing over to implement a new public defender program in that community. The neighborhood was crowded with low-income housing and had become a recruitment zone for juvenile offenders. Mr. Robinson aimed to not only reverse the high rate at which these young offenders grew into a life of adult crime. He wanted his program to influence them to complete their education and embark on a path of higher education that often led to legal lucrative jobs.

"One of the criteria we looked for in selecting you as interns this semester is the fact that you've already overcome a hurdle many of our clients fail to surpass. Coming from a low income family should not cause you shame. In fact, it's a badge of honor. When you sit in your college classrooms surrounded by peers who grew up in middle income and wealthy families, peers who were privileged to attend some of the best high schools in the country, remember, they had a head start. The neighborhood each of you grew up in is a lot like this one, with schools that don't measure up to the government's standard, where students typically rank below average on standardized test. In spite of that background, you're here. Having completed two years of college with a GPA of 3.0 or better, you've proven that you can compete and that you're just as intelligent as your peers who came from more privileged backgrounds. Your mere existence is an inspiration to the clients you will meet during your work experience here."

Mr. Robinson completed his presentation and excused himself from the room. Once again, Karlene addressed the group.

"Okay! You've been well fed and you've rubbed shoulders with the executives around here. A word of advice, remember their names. Address them as Mr. or Ms. unless they invite you to call them by their first name—and they probably will. We're usually informal around the office. I'll take you on a tour of our organization now, and I'll introduce you to the attorneys you'll be working with. Go ahead and pack up. It's late afternoon now, so most of the attorneys should be back from court. Expect to remain with the attorney you're assigned to for the rest of the afternoon. Two interns have been assigned to each attorney. We've gone through the list and paired you up alphabetically. There was only one instance where two people from any one academic institution will be working together—that's with Paul Chambers and Wendy Douglas. Everyone else will be working with someone new."

Wendy's papers missed her leather attaché case and slid to the floor. As she knelt down to pick them up, she regretted that she hadn't taken time to look around at the other interns. Instead, she'd kept her focus riveted on the speaker who was addressing the group. Had Karlene really just said Paul Chambers?

"I'll help you with those." Paul's arms reached out to quickly gather the papers she had scattered on the floor.

She didn't have to look up at his face to identify the owner of those hands and that husky voice. She knew him well. "Thanks," she said, and removed the papers from his hands without making eye contact. She turned her attention to placing them in her attaché case, so she could catch up to the others who were already on their way out the door. She slung the strap over her shoulder and looked up to see Paul holding the door.

He smiled at her.

This time her eyes met his, and she noted that they held sincere joy. Was he happy about this? She couldn't believe this was happening? Everything else about the internship seemed so ideal. Suddenly, her dream was turning into a nightmare. She could not spend the entire semester working with Constance Channing's fiancé.

She politely said, "Thanks again," and hurried past him and caught up with one of the females in the group.

Paul couldn't believe his good fortune. "What a blessing!" he thought. He had known that another student from the college had received the same internship placement but he had no idea it was Wendy. He watched her walking up ahead of him and thought of how well she was wearing that suit. He looked forward to spending time with her each week, away from the college campus—away from Constance. Instantly, a pang of guilt seared his gut. He was engaged to marry Constance. He cared about Constance, he reminded himself. She'd done so much for him, and for that he was grateful. Yet, he could hear his mother advising him that he didn't owe Constance his life.

Karlene beckoned Paul forward as they stopped outside one of the offices. "Wendy, Paul, this is Torrell Norton. We'll leave you here so you can get to know each other."

Wendy and Paul shook hands with Ms. Norton, who didn't ask them to call her by her first name.

Ms. Norton invited them to sit in one of the arm chairs facing her desk, and she returned to her spot behind the desk. She wore a serious look on her face. "All fun and games end here," she said. "Each paper on my desk represents a real person in crisis. At our best, we have the opportunity to turn a youngster's life around and set him or her on a path to social and economic advancement. Worst case scenario, we're a mere bump on the road to destruction: a life of crime spent in and out of prison, leading to death."

Her lips parted into a smile, but she pierced Paul and Wendy with her eyes. "Most of our cases lie somewhere in between." She waved her hand over the files on her desk and commanded them to pull out the handout they'd received regarding confidentiality.

"In a nut shell, you'll learn from those pages that the information you're privy to regarding our clients remains in this office. As you ride the buses and the trains—by whatever means you get here—do not discuss our clients and our situations. You could be sitting beside someone's neighbor, or worst yet, you could be unwittingly divulging information to someone working in the prosecutor's office. Play it safe. Leave the discussion here. If you run into our clients in the neighborhood, greet them, if it's natural and appropriate, but don't allow them to enter a discussion of their case in public."

She looked at Paul and added, "No matter how good looking our clients are," she shifted her focus to Wendy, "or how much they try to kick it to you, we have a no dating policy. Absolutely not. Don't even think about it. Never. No way. We're not having that. Do you understand?"

"Yes," Wendy replied.

"Yes, Ma'am," Paul said.

"I know I might seem like an ogre, but I can't emphasize enough the importance of confidentiality. Our clients' lives depend on it. Any questions?"

Wendy and Paul shook their heads.

"Great. I'd like you to sit at the table over there and read over our policy on confidentiality and then write a report with specific details on how that policy applies to your role here. Keep it short, to the point, and specific. Your finished document will also serve as a writing sample illustrating in what capacity you can help me. I've cleared the table of any files, so you have space to work. Do not examine or expose yourself to any of the files lying around my office. I'll be leaving the room to meet with a client. If I'm not back by the time you're finished, leave your report on my desk. You're not expected to stay beyond your four-hour commitment, so you have an hour remaining. Any questions?"

"No," Wendy and Paul chorused.

"Great!" She smiled genuinely for the first time. "I selected you both because you're students at my alma mater. I look forward to working with you, and I promise you that I won't have you fetching coffee. You'll get substantive work experience while you're here."

She shook their hands again and guided them to the table. Paul and Wendy removed a legal pad from their attaché cases and arranged it on the table along with the handouts and pens. Wendy began reading and highlighting the handout with a pink highlighter.

Ms. Norton gathered some documents from her desk and headed toward the door. "See you next week."

"Bye," Paul replied.

"Nice meeting you," Wendy offered.

Ms. Norton closed the door behind her, but Paul and Wendy felt like they were on display behind the transparent office walls.

Wendy wanted to do the assignment well, but quickly, so she could escape the office before Paul attempted to have a personal discussion with her.

Paul, on the other hand, couldn't wait to talk to Wendy. He wondered whether she had known he would be there. They were sitting on opposite sides of the table. Every now and again, he stole a look at her. He considered her feelings at this moment, and he didn't want to make her upset or uncomfortable. Yes, she had hurt him when she ended their relationship two years ago by going off to Africa when he couldn't afford to go with her. Yet, it was his more recent engagement to Constance that had caused fresh pain. She had not handled their previous confrontations without getting upset, so he resisted the urge to speak to her now. She would lose too much, if his actions caused her to run away tearfully, as she had done when he tried to talk to her after class. He knew this internship was as important to her as it was to him, and he would try not to ruin that for her. In his mind, he prayed for her, for her success, for her peace of mind.

Wendy prayed for herself, asking God to help her to focus and concentrate. She would deal with the matter of Paul Chambers' presence later. At that moment, she just wanted to make a good impression on Ms. Norton.

After reading over her essay one last time, Wendy finally looked across the table at Paul. His eyes met hers and he smiled. How she missed that smile! She felt like she had butterflies in her stomach. Simple pleasure replaced all the trepidation she'd felt about being alone with Paul—knowing he was engaged to Constance. She thought of all the people that might be praying for her and Paul at that very moment. People who wanted them to be reconciled: his mother, her parents, the pastor from their church. Inwardly, she thanked God for answering those prayers and for the peace that set the atmosphere at that moment.

"Are you finished?" she asked him.

"Yes. I was waiting for you."

Her eyes searched his, but she decided that she didn't want answers, or promises about the future. She just wanted to enjoy this moment with him. "Thanks. Do you think Ms. Norton will mind if we read over each other's essays."

Like old times, Paul thought, remembering they would double-check each other's homework assignments while they were in high school. He missed the comfort that came from having a likeminded friend that he could always rely on. "My guess is she won't because we'll be working as a team."

"You're right." She handed him her paper and took his.

They read the essays over in silence, but Paul imagined that Wendy could hear how hard his heart was beating from the thrill of the acceptance she had just shown him. After a few minutes, he said, "It's good, but you used T-H-E-R-E right here. You meant T-H-E-I-R."

"Good eye, man," Wendy said, thanking him. "And you confused your 'its'. If you're using the contraction meaning it is, you need to write I-T apostrophe S."

He gazed into her eyes for a moment. "We wouldn't want Ms. Norton to think we're not up to speed on our grammar."

"You got that right."

They made the corrections and gathered their belongings. Paul held the door open for her as they left the room.

At the receptionist's desk, Paul said, "Good night," but Wendy stopped to ask if she needed a key for the ladies' room.

The receptionist handed her a single key on a wooden key ring.

Paul stood with some of the other interns who were waiting for the elevator.

Wendy waved. When she returned from the ladies' room, she was pleasantly surprised to find him waiting for her. A broad grin spread across her face.

That smile, Paul thought, noticing how Wendy's eyes gleamed. He remembered when she would always smile like that for him. "Ready?" he asked.

"Yes. Thanks for waiting for me."

"Would you expect otherwise?" he asked, and then he realized that the question might lead her to make a remark about his engagement to Constance.

Wendy thought, "I don't know what to expect these days, Paul," but she held her tongue, so as not to ruin the moment.

They boarded the elevator and rode it down to the lobby.

"I'm parked in the garage across the street." Wendy said.

"Me too. It's pricey though, considering we're not getting paid. I've been weighing the option of public transportation."

Wendy nodded. He sounded like her old friend Paul, always frugal. She had wondered if hanging out with Constance, and her showy and extravagant diva-tude, had rubbed off on him. She felt relieved that it hadn't. "Look at it as an investment; not as an expense," she suggested.

"That'll help." He thought of something else to say that would keep them on neutral ground. "How are your parents?"

"They're fine. Thanks for asking. Dad's getting ready to open the new villas."

"Tell him I said congratulations. How does your mother like living in Jamaica?"

"She loves it, but she misses the family here."

"That's expected because your family is so close-knit." He thought of Wendy's family that he'd known so well while they were growing up: her mother, her Aunt Pat and Uncle Trevor, their daughter and her husband, and the twins. They all shared a three-story brick apartment house in New York. He hadn't thought about them in a long time. "How are the twins? They must be big now."

Wendy grinned. "I have pictures." She placed her attaché case on top of her car as they stood beside it. Then she pulled up some pictures on the screen of her cell phone and showed him. As she handed the phone to him, their hands touched and she gasped.

Paul felt certain she could hear his heart pounding. In all their years together, they had been just friends. They hadn't even shared a deep kiss because they meant to honor the commitment they made to God and each other to save themselves for marriage. A kiss, like the one he was imagining at that moment, would only tempt them to go farther.

"I was thinking of going home to see them this weekend." Wendy had been thinking of getting away from him. The weekends were hardest for her. The way Constance always strived to call attention to herself hadn't bothered Wendy before, but now it hurt deeply because she was wearing Paul's engagement ring. At that moment, the sentiment between them was so tender that she expected a hug from him more than she expected an emotional blow.

Paul thought of how much their relationship had changed in the two years since the twins were born. The twins' mother was Wendy's mother's biological cousin, but those two maternal figures lived like sisters, so Wendy called her Aunt Blossom. As they lingered there beside each other, standing next to Wendy's car, Paul thought about the events that happened on the night the twins were born. In many ways, that night had been the beginning of the break-up between him and Wendy.

Wendy had called him in the wee hours of the morning from her father's house. The twins were fine, but Wendy's paternal grandfather had died. As a result, her father would need to leave for Jamaica later that morning. Wendy was devastated when her father didn't return from Jamaica in time to attend her high school graduation in New York. She had prayed for God to bring her father into her life, and when she met him during her senior year of high school, she believed that God had sent him, so that he could be present at her graduation, and that he would walk her down the aisle so she could marry Paul. When he missed her high school graduation, Wendy began to ponder how much she and Paul really knew about God's plan for their lives. Then, impulsively, she used a credit card her father had given her and charged a ticket to Africa where she spent a few weeks that summer. Before she left, Paul had threatened to break up with her. He'd said that if she went without him, he wouldn't be waiting for her when she returned.

She went.

For the first time since that summer, he no longer felt angry at her. Their eyes locked and held, as he inwardly praised God for enabling him to forgive her. All the unforgiveness he had carried in his heart had led him down a path of poor decision making. He started to apologize. "I'm…"

"Yes, I need to go too. Constance is probably waiting for you." She removed her cell phone from his grasp.

He felt a sense of loss and regret, but the mention of Constance's name served as a harsh reality check. He was determined that he would always be a one-woman man, so he needed to close the door on his relationship with Constance before he reopened one with Wendy.

"You're right. We're already going to get caught in the evening rush hour traffic."

"Thanks for walking me to my car."

He wanted to say, "You can always count on me," but that would have been as untrue as it was corny. Yet, he longed for them to have that type of relationship again. "Travel safely," he said instead.

She sat in the car and started the ignition. "Go ahead," she said waving her hand toward where his car was parked. "I'll wait for you to get to yours."

He kept looking back at her as he walked away.

She drove her car over behind his as he was opening up the car door.

"Remember to pray for me," he told her.

She looked at him long and hard. Then finally she said, "Pray for me too," and drove away.

CHAPTER ELEVEN

All student activity groups had their offices in the student recreation center, a tall building with outer walls like mirrors that reflected the sky. On that day, the building shimmered bright blue.

Monique flung open the door to the club room where the African and American Students Union met. "I can't stand her," she declared, exhaling a grunt of frustration as she entered the room.

"Who?" asked the woman seated nearest to the door.

"Wendy Douglas." Monique sat at a table where a group of young women were playing the card game Uno. The club room was a popular place to pass the time between classes. Some students ate their lunch there; others hung out listening to music, or simply socializing. Sometimes, they would get stuck just hanging out and never make it to class.

"Don't you mean Holy Roller?" another asked.

"The one and only. When is she going to wake up and realize that most people don't care about her religion? I mean, there we were in class taking about enterprise versus exploitation in music videos, and there she comes with her Bible-thumping self. I wasn't even trying to hear her and her Scripture quoting, and I know I'm not the only one." Monique extended her neck forward and circled back to emphasize her annoyance.

"What did your professor say?" asked one of her friends. "I have a class with that gospel singing Paul Chambers and our professor shuts him down completely when he begins to talk about his religion. Professor Willoughby is just not having that."

"Paul is in my class too, and it was like he and Wendy were tag teaming me today—again. But that's the last straw. Wait until I tell Constance how Wendy has been trying to push up on her man."

"Tell the truth," Sergio said, as he exited the inner office of the club room.

Monique hadn't realized that Sergio was already there. When she hadn't seen him in the outer office, she assumed that he hadn't yet arrived from class. The inner office door was usually kept closed and accessed by officers of the club who had to sign out and return the key to the administration room each time they used it.

"I always call it like I see it and I see Paul and Wendy being really chummy. I saw them holding hands in the hallway. The funniest part was how after a moment, she turned and ran away from him. She must have seen me coming because she knows I'm tight with Constance."

"We sorority sisters have got to look out for each other," the young woman sitting beside her agreed, and they both made a hand signal indicating their solidarity.

Sergio resisted the urge to launch a full scale defense on Wendy's behalf. He would have to find out from her later if there was any truth to Monique's report. For now, he'd simply force them to switch subjects by calling the club meeting to order. He looked around the room. "I see we have a quorum. Let's start the meeting."

One of the women seated at the table with Monique got up and distributed copies of the agenda.

"Thanks."

She blushed as Sergio smiled at her and his eyes seemed to linger on her longer than necessary.

Monique rolled her eyes thinking Sergio was such a flirt. If he wasn't almost a straight 'A' student, she would have no respect for him.

"This meeting shall come to order. As your Acting President until the upcoming elections, I'd like to extend a warm welcome to each of you, on behalf of all the officers who enjoyed serving during the last school year. It was a fun year—and we continue to be known for our parties—but more importantly, we were involved in social change in the community. Last year, we returned in the aftermath of a tragedy that claimed the lives of three young adults in this state. The tragedy highlighted an unspoken crisis. It showed how much young black men, and women, just entering adulthood, are at risk of losing their lives because of violent crime. Many of us identified with the victims from last summer's senseless killings. Like us, they were upwardly mobile, hoping to make better lives for themselves and their families by attaining a college education. Our club teamed up with the black fraternities and sororities on campus to dedicate a scholarship in their honor. At the awards banquet in October, we will be able to present a two thousand dollar check to the inaugural scholarship winner."

Monique scribbled a few words on a piece of paper and slid it on the desk in front of him.

He smiled charmingly at her.

"I'd be completely lost without you," he said, looking into her eyes before turning his attention to the entire group. "Our Acting Vice President Monique Williams has just reminded me of the school supplies we have committed to donating to students at the school where the incident took place. We'll need a committee to get on that immediately." He tore a sheet of paper from his writing pad. "I'm circulating a sign-up sheet for volunteers who will secure the donations, shop for any other items needed, and contact the school's principal to make the presentation."

"Committed people only," Monique interjected. "We don't baby-sit or mop up after committee members. If you say you're going to do something, we expect that you'll make your best effort to do it. Otherwise, don't sign up for the responsibility. Thanks." She chimed in her expression of gratitude.

Sergio nodded.

A calendar of events for the upcoming school year was drafted. It included two parties each semester and a fall and spring awards dinner.

"I'd like to add an event," Monique suggested. "If you'll yield the floor for a moment, Sergio, I'd like to explain."

He nodded.

"Many of you have already completed your semester abroad at the University of Ghana and may be familiar with the music video contest they had among the student body there. The contest challenges producers to elevate the content of their videos, making them less sexy and more socially conscious. I'd argue that both qualities have value. Anyway, our faculty advisor suggests that if there is adequate student interest, we could host a similar competition here."

There were many nods and comments of approval.

"Once again, we'll need a planning committee." Sergio tore off another sheet of paper and headed it, "Music video contest."

"Only sign up if you mean it," Monique reminded the group. "We're going to need people to plan and promote the event, to recruit entries and judges, to secure donations for the prizes. My vision is to have an exec from BET involved. Perhaps, the winning video could be aired on cable television."

There was a murmur of excitement among the group as many volunteers signed up to be involved with that project.

Sergio accomplished much during that meeting, but it went on longer than he had expected and he ended up having to rush to his next class. It wasn't until late that evening that he finally connected with Wendy.

He cooked a quick dinner, but before he went take a shower, he sent her a text message to find out if she had eaten yet.

"Nope. Starving." She texted him back. "Cook?"

"Yes. Want some?"

"I'm there."

"LOL." He laughed out loud. She hadn't even asked what he cooked. He knew Wendy loved to eat more than she loved to cook and would probably eat whatever he made. He took a quick shower and changed into a fresh pair of jeans, button-down shirt, and sandals. He was tempted to leave the shirt open as he flexed his muscles in front of the mirror, but that attempt at seduction would work on every other woman on campus before it worked on Wendy.

He heard a knock at the door.

"Just a minute," he yelled and changed into a long-sleeve t-shirt.

She walked past him the moment he opened the door. "Feed me, Sergio. Is your bathroom decent, or should I wash my hands at the kitchen sink?"

He shook his head. "I keep a clean house."

She stopped long enough to smile at him. "Yes. That's one of the things I hear the women love about you." She slipped away to the bathroom before he could respond.

Sergio's cooking skills, both in and out of the kitchen—along with his clean-up skills—made most women consider him a good catch. He knew Wendy didn't share their perspective.

"So, what are we eating tonight, Dear?" Wendy teased, as she returned.

"Oh, you got jokes. Don't start something you can't finish," Sergio said seriously, wondering why he felt so much love for this woman. He could have invited so many other women over. Many would have been happy to repay him for that meal with their bodies. Instead, he had invited the most prudish person he knew. Perhaps, he hoped some of her purity would one day rub off on him.

Wendy removed a plate from his cupboard and helped herself to fried fish and vegetables. "I never waste good food. I will finish what I started," she said, purposely misinterpreting his comment.

"Funny." He took a plate for himself and filled it up.

"Oh. I thought you already ate," Wendy said, with her mouth full of food. She sat on a stool.

"Carrot juice?" Sergio asked.

"Yes. Please."

He brought over a tray with his plate and the glasses of orange-colored drink.

Wendy took a gulp. "Thanks so much. You saved my life."

"Again," Sergio replied, chuckling. "It seems like I'm always doing that."

Wendy frowned at him, as she thought of the times she'd literally run into his arms when she thought the heartache she was feeling over Paul would kill her. "You're right. I need to stop that."

"Really. I don't mind."

Sergio's smile revealed perfect teeth. He had his long dreadlocks pulled back in a ponytail, but he was all man, thought Wendy. One hundred percent male hunting down the female species. If only he could remain committed to a relationship with just one woman, that woman would be blessed to have him.

"You got a date tonight?" Wendy asked.

Sergio nodded. He always had a date on a Friday night. Getting together with a warm-bodied woman was his way of unwinding, after a week of studying hard and working hard. "And you? There are a few parties tonight. Why don't you go have some fun, instead of sitting in your room praying for that jerk to come to his senses?"

Wendy almost choked on her food. She literally did stay in her room sometimes praying for herself and Paul. But on Sergio's lips, it sounded like an act of futility. She smiled as she thought about the time she and Paul had spent together on the first day of their internship. She hadn't told anyone about that. To her, that was proof that God was hearing and answering her prayers.

"I should do something different tonight," she replied.

"Good."

"I should spend that time praying for you."

"There you go again. You got jokes? Why are you so happy this evening?"

"God is just great, Sergio. You really need to surrender your life to him."

If anyone else had said those words, Sergio would have ended the conversation. But he cared about Wendy so much that he ignored that comment and listened to what else she had to say.

"I started the semester dreading having to face Paul and Constance, with that big fat engagement ring on her finger. Now, I'm convinced that we're going to get back together."

"Really? Did he tell you that?"

"No. I got that information from a higher authority."

Sergio thought for a moment before he spoke. "Be careful what you do. You know those Greeks look out for each other. Constance and her sorority sisters have their eye on you. Don't go off on any secret rendezvous with Paul. They probably won't remain secret for long."

"I wouldn't do that—not until I know for sure that he has broken up with her."

"That's what you're expecting."

"Yes."

"Well the last I heard, she just hired a wedding planner."

"Where did you hear that?"

"Let's just say, I know a lot of women, and they are always talking—kind of like you." Sergio chuckled, hoping to take the painful edge off the news he just told her.

Wendy was thoughtful, but quiet. "Have you heard that Paul and I got placed at the same internship?" she asked after a while.

"Did you? And did you go running from the room when he walked in?"

"No. What kind of weakling do you think I am?"

They both knew that she had literally run from Paul on more than one occasion.

"Okay. You'd never do that," Sergio said sarcastically.

"Not anymore, anyway. I'm telling you, Sergio, prayer really works. It caught me off-guard when I found out that Paul and I would be working together, but after that, it was like we were old friends again. I enjoyed being with him. It felt like old times. There is no tangible reason why things were so much better, but I know a whole lot of people have been praying for us to get back together. Didn't your momma ever tell you that prayer changes things?"

"My momma didn't know nothing about prayer," Sergio responded, using double negatives for emphasis.

"Sorry." Wendy realized that she didn't know Sergio at all, outside of his college life. She dared to add, "Your mommy wasn't Christian." It was meant as a question.

"She wasn't religious at all. She taught me self reliance. That's the only way you're going to make it in this world."

Wendy prayed for God to give her the right words to say. She decided to ask the question, "Was she a single mother?"

"She wasn't much of a mother. I think she was a victim of domestic violence. I don't remember my time with her too well. What I do remember was the hell I went through after I got taken from her and put in foster care."

"I'm sorry."

"Don't be. I'm a better man for it. It taught me to work hard for what I want. It helped me to see that I don't need to depend on anybody. I can take care of myself. I've been doing so for many years."

"You do a really good job of it too," Wendy complimented him sincerely.

"Thanks. I really care about you, Wendy. I don't want to see you let that jerk hurt you again."

Wendy thought about the ways Sergio had shown her that he really cared about her. She had taken his friendship for granted, not ever questioning why he did the things he did. "Why do you take such good care of me, Sergio?"

"I really don't know," he said, getting up from the table and starting to clean up.

"I know."

"Really now? Let's hear it."

"Because you're a godsend. God knew how much I'd need a friend like you, so he put you in my life for that reason."

Sergio just shook his head and took the dishes back to the kitchen.

"He knew you would need me too."

"If you say so." Sergio's tone of voice made it clear that he didn't agree. After all, he had just told her that he needed no one. "I'm giving you a bottle of carrot juice to take back to the dorm with you."

Wendy brought over her dishes. "As always, this was delicious. Do you have enough food left for your date?"

"This isn't for her. I don't plan to bring her here tonight."

"Well, be safe out there... wherever you'll be."

"Yes, ma'am."

She felt like he was dismissing her, but she understood that he needed to get ready for his date. Perhaps he regretted that he had opened up to her so much, she thought. He always presented himself as a man of steel.

She hugged him. "I will be praying for you."

"You do that."

After she left, Sergio had the haunting feeling that he needed to pray for himself.

CHAPTER TWELVE

There was a lot of activity on her floor when Wendy returned to the dorm. She bumped into one of the girls from her liturgical dance group who was leaving the kitchen.

"Hey girl," said Kim. "Where you been?"

"Where you been?" Wendy returned her question. "Hanging with your boyfriend?"

"We've been wondering if you have a new boyfriend. You've been so scarce." Kim walked Wendy to her room.

"I started my internship on top of all the work I've had to do for classes. These professors don't play. We hit the ground running."

"I hear you. We still need to schedule a rehearsal once a week like we did last semester."

"For real." Wendy didn't argue. She enjoyed their rehearsals. The praise music and dance were relaxing. They kept her body in motion praising the Lord.

Kim closed the door behind them and sat down in Wendy's room and commenced eating her food. "Want some?"

Wendy shook her head. "I just ate." She placed the plastic bag with the carrot juice Sergio had given her into her mini-refrigerator.

"What are you doing tonight?"

"Just chilling."

"Donna and I are going party hopping with the other girls. Come with us."

"I'll be partying right here with the Holy Ghost, and you know the Holy Ghost party don't stop," Wendy said, bopping her shoulders up and down.

Kim rolled her eyes at her. "Come on. It'll be fun. Do something different for a change."

"I'll have my fun right here, thank you very much. Don't get me started on why ya'll shouldn't be going to those parties. Your body is the Lord's temple. You need to keep it holy. All that rump shaking and booty bumping you'll be doing at those parties will mess up your sanctified dance ministry. God can use an anointed dancer to win souls for His kingdom."

"Lighten up, girl. It's Friday night. They call you Holy Roller for a reason."

"The name doesn't bother me. I take it as a compliment."

"Wendy, you are one of a kind." Kim got up and headed for the door. "I'm young, free, and single, and I'm going to have some fun tonight."

"Good for you. Later."

Wendy locked her door. She would have to go down the hallway to take a shower in the shared bathroom, but she would wait for the party-goers and bar-hoppers to leave. The dorm would be quite empty soon, as was the norm on a Friday night.

For Wendy, Friday night turned out to be a good time to fast and seek God by reading the Bible and praying about things she didn't make enough time for during the rest of the week. She turned her radio on with the volume low. She kept it tuned to the local gospel station. She closed her eyes and listened to the lyrics of the music.

One song ended, and shortly after she started listening, another song began. Wendy noticed a pattern in the music. Each song was about forgiveness and reconciliation. By the second stanza Wendy realized that the singer, Kevin LeVar, was actually praying as he sung the song A Heart That Forgives, and she knelt down beside her bed.

As Wendy listened to the lyrics sung to a slow melody, she kept her eyes closed. She knew the Bible said that the Holy Spirit makes intercession for her when she knew not what she ought to pray. This song did just that. She needed this: a heart that forgives like Jesus did. So did Paul. So did Sergio. She prayed with each of them in mind.

Paul was her closest friend, the one she'd known the longest who had hurt her the most. The pain felt as fresh as when she first learned of his engagement to Constance.

As she listened to the song, she prayed that she would truly forgive him. "Yes, Lord," Wendy said out loud. "Help me."

The song described the private pain some people carry inside them and never tell anyone. "This one is for Sergio, Lord," Wendy prayed. "You know the life he's lived, and the pain he's suffered."

She continued praying, "Touch Sergio's heart, Lord. Help him to know that you're his Savior too. Replace the unforgiveness he feels toward his mother and those who abandoned him. Replace it with the love of Jesus. Help us, please, Lord."

Tears streamed down Wendy's face as she prayed, "Jesus. Help me,

Jesus. Free us, Lord, from the pain of the past. Help us to live our lives to please you. Free us from a reaction to pain that causes us to make bad decisions—decisions that hurt us even more."

The song ended, but Wendy continued in her prayer.

"Lord, help us to let it go. We can't do it on our own." She sobbed again and wiped away the tears streaming down her face. She remained on her knees, but without opening her eyes, she reached over and turned off the radio. "Lord, I let go of the pain Paul has caused me, and I ask you to forgive me for the pain that I have caused him. Help him to let it go, Lord, and help us to live like we mean it, in Jesus' name."

Wendy grew silent. She thought of the Bible verse, "Be still and know that I am God," and she did that for long while.

Eventually, she got up and picked up her Bible, which she kept lying open to Psalm 91 in her room. She flipped to the back of the Bible and searched the concordance for the word forgive.

She turned the pages to Matthew, chapter six, and was reminded that the Lord's prayer includes these lines: Forgive us our trespasses, as we forgive those who trespass against us.

The two verses that followed the prayer talked even more about forgiveness. She read verses fourteen and fifteen.

"For if you forgive men their trespasses, your heavenly Father will also forgive you. But if you do not forgive men their trespasses, neither will your Father forgive your trespasses."

She had read these words before, but had forgotten about them as she wallowed in her misery over Paul's engagement to Constance.

"Lord, I forgive Paul. From this day forward, please help me to treat him like I mean that."

CHAPTER THIRTEEN

Paul sat in the car outside Constance's apartment building waiting for her to come outside. He had called and told her he was on his way and she promised she would be ready, but he wasn't surprised that he had to wait. Constance lived up to her reputation as a diva by taking the time to make a fashion statement. She never repeated an outfit. Perhaps, she re-wore an item, but never in the same way. A long, rectangular cloth would one day serve as a scarf and be reinvented into a belt with another outfit. She had a penchant for high-heeled boots and was known to run up stairs in them, if she needed to. She changed her hairstyle often, leaving spectators to guess which one was her natural hair. She wore wigs, weaves, and hats, depending on the statement she wanted to make.

The door to her building opened and the doorman stepped out. Constance emerged from behind him wearing trademark knee-high boots. Her strides were elegant and unhurried, her hips swaying provocatively as she extended each long leg clad in a pair of tight black pants. As she got closer to the car, Paul was struck by the length of her hair tonight. Constance lifted her right hand and repositioned her hair over her right shoulder. Strands of thick, straight, jet black hair hung to her waist.

"Wow!" Paul exclaimed, as she sat in the car beside him. "You should be on stage tonight."

Lips bright red with lipstick parted as she smiled at him. "I enjoy working behind the scenes. You know that."

Paul noticed that she wore her eyelashes longer and fuller than usual this evening. "True. But you also love the spotlight."

"Is anything wrong with that?" Constance asked. Lately, Paul's tone always sounded critical to her. She wondered if he was comparing her to Wendy.

Paul admired her beauty. He knew Constance spent a lot of time on her appearance and each new image she created complimented her God-given good looks. Tonight, though, he felt her emphasis lay in the wrong place. Whenever he and Wendy prepared to witness for the Lord, through singing or some other means, they took time to prepare themselves spiritually by praying and reading their Bibles. During the time Paul had been working with Constance, he had often invited her to read and pray with him. Sometimes, she joined him. At other times, she found so many other things to do that she didn't seem to have time.

He started the car and drove off, feeling unprepared for the event that they were driving to. He should have been excited. He was going to be performing on stage that night with some of the most well-known gospel music singers. One of the performers had canceled at the last minute, and Constance managed to secure Paul's spot as the replacement. He was even getting paid—well.

"Are you okay?" Constance asked.

"Fine," Paul replied.

"You seem a little on edge. You're not nervous are you? I know you better than that."

"I'm fine really," Paul insisted impatiently. "I just need a moment of quiet reflection."

He felt guilty. Constance hadn't done anything wrong. He was the one who had proposed to the wrong woman. He was the one who had let his anger and unwillingness to forgive stand between him and Wendy.

He thought of Wendy, his forever love. Had she been the one supporting him tonight, they would have prayed together. Given the nature of this opportunity, they probably would have fasted and just asked God to save every unsaved soul who attended the concert. At least he had opened his Bible during the hour he sat in the car waiting for Constance to get dressed. He had to keep starting over the same Scripture because his mind kept drifting to Wendy. How he longed to be with her now, instead of with Constance.

There was that guilty feeling again, gnawing at his conscience. He didn't want to hurt Constance. She had made his music career. Yes, God had gifted him with a good singing voice and a talent for playing more than one musical instrument, but it was Constance's connections that launched him from obscurity. Being the boyfriend—now fiancé—of Bill Channing's daughter opened doors. He couldn't deny that.

He hadn't set out to build a music career over the last two years. He had just wanted to have a little more money. During their last year of high school, after Wendy had met her rich father and he started spending money on her, Paul hadn't been able to compete. When she spent thousands on a ticket to Africa, on a whim, and he couldn't afford to follow, that had been the deepest insult. So, he accepted each opportunity Constance told him about, and was pleased that they paid more than he made working retail. Eventually, he left the band that he'd started out playing with when he first arrived at the college. Since he'd received the Stellar and Dove awards, those band members now considered it an honor to play with him. He owed all that to Constance.

Call it self-defense against Paul's resistance to her, but Constance felt particularly dissatisfied with their relationship tonight. She had been in a series of monogamous relationships, but this was the first time that her boyfriend was not also her lover. Ironically, he was the one she pursued for marriage.

She had been called a spoiled brat, and she was used to getting her own way. But her critics would never have guessed that all she really wanted was a family who loved her. The more she had gotten to know Paul, the more she'd convinced herself that Paul would provide that security she always longed for. He was a man of integrity, striving to please the Lord. A Bible believing, ten commandment following man was hard to find—in any age group. She felt lucky to have been the only woman to hold his attention and dominate his time since they'd met each other on campus. She enjoyed being with him, but at times like this, she needed for them to talk more.

He always seemed to leave her to guess at his feelings. Right now, she suspected that he was thinking about Wendy.

"We should have invited her," Constance said.

"Who?" Paul asked, glancing at her.

"Wendy Douglas. Perhaps you and she could have done a duet."

Paul grunted. He wondered how Constance knew he had been thinking about Wendy.

"You seem to enjoy working together: on stage at the club fair, at your internship, why not here?"

"Who told you about the internship?"

"The more important question is: When were you going to tell me?"

"After the show. I didn't see the point in us getting in an argument right before the show began."

"How could you keep that as a secret from me? It makes me wonder what else is going on between the two of you."

"Nothing is going on between Wendy and me. Wendy and I are just friends."

"Isn't that what we are? I may be wearing your engagement ring, but you have never really kissed me, Paul. I mean a deep passionate kiss. We've never made love. We spend a lot of time together, but there is no intimacy between us. So to say Wendy is just a friend doesn't tell me that I mean any more to you than she does."

Paul glanced over at her, but mostly kept his eye on the road. He felt that this was not a conversation they needed to have before the show. It would leave them feeling emotionally upset. He planned to break off the engagement with Constance and he expected her to cry. With all the makeup she had on, her face would be a mess. That would make her even more upset.

"It's better to wait," he said out loud.

"Does she mean more to you than I do, Paul?"

"I don't think it's a good idea for me to answer that now. Please. Let's talk about it after the show."

"You've said enough." Constance turned her head away from him and gazed out the window. They were in the heart of the city now, and the car whizzed by monotonous blocks of tall buildings.

"The show must go on." Constance repeated that mantra again and again. Each time she used a different intonation. She pulled down the visor so she could see herself in the mirror and practice a variety of facial expressions. She was good at hiding her true feelings and putting on a happy face. She'd had many opportunities to practice. For most of her life, she had put on a happy face each time her father didn't show up for her birthday, graduation ceremony, or sporting events. She had gotten so good at pretending that she sometimes genuinely enjoyed herself. She hoped that this would be one of those nights.

She felt relief as Paul finally parked the car in the parking garage next to the stadium.

He turned to her and asked, "Are you going to be okay? We don't have to go inside, if you don't want to."

"Are you kidding? My reputation is on the line, not just yours. I had to pull a lot of strings to get you in here at the last minute. I'm not about to let any of those people down." As she spoke, she opened her car door and climbed out.

Paul felt more concerned about her feelings than her reputation. He had not expected her to display such emotional strength. He got out of the car and reached down to retrieve his saxophone from the back seat.

"You won't need that," Constance said, walking around to Paul's side of the car. Her facial expression reflected the bossiness conveyed by her tone of voice.

"I haven't told you what song I'll be performing."

"No. I told you that the atmosphere for this event is upbeat. Contemporary Christian and foot-stomping gospel music. Later for your moaning and groaning on that saxophone."

Paul opened his mouth to respond, but changed his mind. He recognized her behavior for what it was: self-defense and retaliation against him because of his feelings for Wendy.

He did not put back the saxophone.

They stood toe to toe for a moment just staring into each other's eyes.
Paul reached for her hand and said, "I'm sorry."
Before he could get the words out, she held up her open hand like a stop sign before his face, and then she walked away.
He followed her into the building.

Most of the songs in the show were up-tempo, just as Constance had predicted. She spent the time backstage, cheerfully mingling with the performers and the stage hands. She didn't discriminate. She enjoyed meeting the 'little people' in the entertainment world just as much as the celebrities. Sometimes people recognized her as Bill Channing's daughter, but she never introduced herself in that manner.

Paul sat in a corner with his head bowed. He tried to pray, on and off, but he wasn't at peace tonight. He knew he couldn't hide his true feelings from God. God knew he longed to be with Wendy. He could hear Constance's laughter. She seemed to be laughing a lot. Her personality suited the entertainment industry, Paul decided. His did not. He remembered how defensive he had gotten once when Wendy's father suggested that he would excel at a music career if he chose to have one. He remembered responding by telling Wendy's father that a music career was not in God's plan for his life.

He wondered what had happened to that plan—the plan that he and Wendy had envisioned that God had for their lives together.

Wendy had deviated from that plan after the disappointment she suffered when her father missed her high school graduation. Had he sold out on that plan for a few extra dollars? He thought for a moment before concluding that his motives could not be explained that simply. The extra money satisfied the inadequacy he had felt when Wendy's father entered her life and started lavishing money on her, but it didn't explain all the choices that led to him being engaged to Constance.

"Paul Chambers."

The shout of his name roused him from his introspection.

He and Constance responded simultaneously.

"He's over here," she said.

"I'm here," he answered, and stood up and lifted up his saxophone.

Constance walked over to him and smoothed the lapel of his jacket. "Stay upbeat out there now," she suggested, and kissed him lightly on the lips. "There is a party in here tonight; not a funeral."

Paul walked away from her and resisted the urge to go in the opposite direction which led outdoors. He felt like a puppet on Constance Channing's string. She had molded his public image, telling him how to dress and what to wear when he was performing. He yielded to her expertise, and was grateful that she had steered him on an upward journey that culminated when he won the Best New Artist Awards.

Usually, she left the choice of music up to him. Her comments irked him.

The spotlight shone on him, and he closed his eyes, willing lines of frustration away from his brows. As he closed his eyes, he saw Wendy's face. He opened them again and stared out at the crowd. He longed to release his emotions by singing a soulful ballad, but he hadn't rehearsed with the band in advance. Constance merely assured him that they knew his hit songs.

He nodded his head to the crowd and placed the mouthpiece of the saxophone against his lips. He played a few lines of a significantly slower version of his hit song. The rendition was mournful. Then suddenly, he pointed to the band, and he snapped his fingers as they picked up the pace.

He should have been flattered when the crowd, thousands thick, started to sing the song. Yet, not even their cheers could lighten his mood. He stopped singing and pointed the microphone in their direction. After they'd sung a few lines without him, he said, "Praise the Lord!" He raised his voice into a shout, "Praise the Lord, everybody!" Then he bellowed melodiously, "Let everything that has breath praise the Lord. Praise the Lord."

The crowd screamed and cheered. Paul kept on praising God. By the end of his performance, he felt chastened, but satisfied, that his focus was back in the right place. This wasn't about him and his feelings. He was there to praise the name of Jesus. He thought of the scriptural basis he had found to justify his music career to himself. He had read in the Bible, in the third chapter of John, verses fourteen and fifteen, "And as Moses lifted up the serpent in the wilderness, even so must the Son of Man be lifted up, that whoever believes in Him should not perish but have eternal life." Paul's goal was clearly expressed by the song writer who penned the lyrics to the hymn, "Lift the precious Savior up, 'til he speaks from eternity. And I, if I be lifted up on the earth, will draw all men unto Me." Paul resolved not to ever again let his mood stand in the way of praising God.

Constance applauded him as he returned back stage. "You were great!"

Paul humbly accepted compliments from some better-known gospel singers. Then he moved closer to Constance and whispered, "Ready to go."

"No. The show is not even over."

Paul hesitated then said, "I'm ready."

"Well, I'm not. The radio station is having an after party. You may want to join me. You never know who you'll meet that could be useful to you in the future."

This idea of a person's usefulness didn't sit well with Paul. It didn't run parallel with what the Bible said about taking care of the least, the neediest, those who had nothing to offer.

He shook his head at Constance. "I'll pass. I brought you here, and I'd feel a lot better if you let me take you home."

Constance's heart lurched as she heard the gentleness in Paul's voice. It reminded her that he was a nice guy, and that's what she loved most about him. But leaving with him now would only make her cry.

"Don't worry about me, Paul." She winked at him. "I'm older than you, remember? I'll get a ride home with someone else."

Paul frowned at her. "Let me take you home."

"No. Really, I'll be okay. This is one of Daddy's stations. I know people. Worst case scenario, I'll call for a chauffeur." Constance took a couple steps backward then turned on her heels and left the room.

As Paul headed for the exit, he could hear her laughter coming from another room.

CHAPTER FOURTEEN

As the semester progressed, Paul never officially broke up with Constance, and Constance continued to flaunt her engagement ring. Both of them immersed themselves in the hectic pace of college life. There were books to read, papers to write, jobs to maintain, and countless social activities. The music video contest promoted by the African and American Students Union captured many students' attention, as they took time to conceptualize, choreograph, and record their entries. The university also held forums for students to watch and discuss the presidential debates.

Sergio won the on-campus election for president of the student government, and he began to study Senator Obama's oratory style.

Wendy felt more comfortable around Paul when she saw him during classes, or they ran into each other on campus.

Each week, Paul looked forward to the time he spent with Wendy at their internship. Their work was substantive, just as attorney Torrell Norton had promised. Ms. Norton asked them to interview one of her juvenile clients and do a case study of the mitigating circumstances that may have led him to commit a violent crime. Her caseload was heavy and her other job duties too plentiful to give her time to move beyond the more visible facts. She explained to Paul and Wendy that she had observed through the years that the criminal defense system dealt harshly with black boys and girls. She advocated reform, and believed that because of their youth, every single one of her juvenile clients deserved a second chance.

One assignment was to help identify an alternative to incarceration for a thirteen-year-old boy.

"Paul, Wendy, this is Dré." Ms. Norton introduced them to a towering teenager with large bright eyes.

"What's up?" Dré tilted his head back and forth in acknowledgement.

His posture conveyed toughness, but Wendy felt drawn to the innocence she saw in his baby-face. "Hi," she responded to his greeting with a smile.

"What's up, man?" Paul said and shook the youngster's hand.

"They are the ones I was telling you about," Ms. Norton continued by way of introduction. "You'll be seeing a lot of Paul and Wendy. I'm asking them to escort you to court and accompany you to some of the other meetings we're setting up for you. They are going to help you get to the places you need to be, on time."

"I'll be there when I get there," Dré retorted unsmilingly.

"Oh yeah? You better fix that attitude, young man. Otherwise, I won't need any help trying to keep up with you. You'll be locked up behind bars."

"Whatever."

Ms. Norton shook her head. She was accustomed to being disrespected by the very clients she was trying to help. They were always on the defensive, at first. But eventually, they warmed up to her when they realized that she was really on their side. She left Paul and Wendy to get to know Dré.

Wendy sat down with a legal pad and pen, ready to take notes. "Is Dré your full name, or is it short for something else?"

"The name's Dré."

Wendy smiled at him, but he didn't smile back. "Cool," she said, and glanced over at Paul, hoping he would chime in.

Paul's approach was intentionally different. He looked around the office space that had been furnished to appeal to adolescent interests. While Wendy tried to connect with Dré, Paul reached for a basketball that was on the floor.

Dré's eyes followed Wendy's line of vision.

As soon as his eyes met Paul's, Paul threw the ball to him. "You play ball, man?" Paul asked.

Dré tilted his head again, giving a slight nod. He threw the ball back so that it bounced once between them and then he turned away.

Paul's eyes implored Wendy for a prayer. It was a look that others might not have noticed, but Wendy clearly understood. She said a silent prayer that they'd be able to connect with, and be a positive influence, on Dré.

Paul took a chance, judging from the youngster's height that he played ball. "I hear you be hooping on the basketball court. We should play some time." Paul's sense of humor kicked in. "You and me shooting hoops on the basketball court. We'd be like… We'd be like Kobe and LeBron. Watch this." He started dribbling the ball toward the hoop that was hung on the wall. He exaggerated his movements intending to be humorous. "He shoots. He scores. Slam-dunk!" Paul turned to face Dré. "In your face, boy."

Dré shook his head, but his lips wore the hint of a smile. "Stupid," he said under his breath.

"You got game?" Paul challenged Dré with a silly grin on his face. "Come on now. Show me what you got."

Paul's antics broke the ice, as they'd prayed it would. He chatted with Dré for a while, working questions based on the information they needed to gather into a casual conversation.

His effectiveness impressed Wendy. Occasionally, she scribbled down a number or something specific that Dré said, but she did so discreetly. Paul developed a good rapport with Dré, and Wendy didn't want her note-taking to cause Dré to become self conscious and stop talking.

After Dré left, Ms. Norton allowed Paul and Wendy to read through the file she'd prepared for Dré's case.

The more Wendy read about the crime Dré was accused of committing, the more shocked she became. "I don't believe this for a minute. Not that kid."

She and Paul sat side by side at the circular table in Ms. Norton's office. Ms. Norton was working busily at her desk.

"Why?" she asked Wendy. "What did you observe about Dré that makes you think he is innocent?"

"Well, once he warmed up to us, he seemed like a really nice kid. Polite. Great sense of humor. He even held the door open for me when we were leaving the room. And when I told him, we'd see him soon, he called me Ma'am."

Ms. Norton laughed out loud. "What did you think of him, Paul?"

"He has a chip on his shoulder, which isn't unusual for a kid his age. He grew up without his father; so did I. As the oldest of six children, he expected to be the man of the house, but his mother brought different men around at different times, and they all tried to rule him. As a result, he maintains a lot of anger."

"You learned all that from that conversation, out there, just now?" Wendy marveled because she had been with Paul and Dré the entire time, but she hadn't gleaned all of that information.

Paul smiled. "Dré and I speak the same language. Some things he said outright. The rest I deduced because I can relate to him—except for the part about his mother and the men. My mother never brought any other man into the house after my father died. To a great extent, she allowed me to be the man of the house. But I can imagine that had I been in Dré's situation, I'd have had some serious problems with my mother and her men."

"I see," Ms. Norton said, pleased with the way her interns had handled their assignment.

Wendy smiled at Paul. She felt proud of him. She didn't feel threatened by the fact that he'd accomplished more than she had on this assignment. They were a team. If he excelled, so did she, and vice versa. That's the way they'd been all their lives, except for the past two years. It felt good to be on the same team once again.

"Well, a word of caution to you both," Ms. Norton said. "Our role is to defend Dré, but we recognize that he could be both. His anger could have led him to commit the crime, but that would not erase the fact that he is a nice kid, just as you think he is. These children have such rough lives that sometimes the circumstances their own parents place them in breed crime."

Wendy and Paul nodded.

"Next week, when you go to pick him up at his house, keep your eyes open. Don't be afraid, but be cautious and wise. Wendy, wear a pair of slacks and walking shoes. I need you to get him to court on time, so the judge won't issue a warrant for his arrest due to his absence. Once his court appearance is over, I need you to take him home, so he won't wander the streets and be picked up by a truant officer."

"What if he goes back out after we leave?" Wendy asked.

"Then, that's on him. But it'll be afternoon by the time you get back to his house, closer to the time he'd get out of school."

Again they nodded.

"Are you familiar with his neighborhood?"

"I am," said Paul. "I can picture the building."

"Good. Here is a stipend for transportation. You'll also have to pay Dré's way. Bring me some receipts."

"We will. Thank you." Paul accepted an envelope from her hand.

"That's it for today."

They looked at the clock on the wall and noted that it was early.

"I know you've only been here for a couple hours, but next week, you'll be putting in extra time. Take back a couple of those hours now. We can't pay you, but we do want to be careful not to ask too much."

"We're happy to do it," Wendy said.

"Good. See you next week." With that remark, Ms. Norton turned to her computer and started typing.

Paul and Wendy packed up their belongings and left.

On the morning of Dré's court date, Paul and Wendy met each other in the college's parking lot. Wendy drove her car, and they parked in the lot near to the office. From there, they briskly walked the blocks to Dré's apartment building. The building looked vacant and abandoned, but it appeared to be the right address. The front door opened without a key because the lock was broken. Paul and Wendy looked around before they walked in. Dré supposedly lived on the top floor of this apartment walk-up, but the staircase was cracked and looked like it was in danger of falling down.

"I'm not going up those stairs," Wendy whispered to Paul.

"Go ahead now. I got your back," Paul replied.

"That's all good, but who's going to catch me if these stairs collapse? You're joking right?"

"Right," Paul answered, chuckling softly. Even in severe circumstances, Paul maintained a sense of humor. "Let's go back outside," he suggested.

They looked up at the windows from the sidewalk downstairs. The windows of the apartment they guessed that Dré lived in had no lights on.

"I'm going to call him." Paul took out his cell phone and dialed Dré's number. On the third try, a sleepy-sounding woman answered the phone. Paul explained to her who they were and their purpose for being there.

"Dré, drag your lazy behind out the bed and go to court before they lock you up."

Paul held the phone away from his ears so Wendy could also hear the woman, who they guessed might be Dré's mother, shout to her son.

"He's coming," she told Paul, lowering her voice. Then, without waiting for his response, she hung up the phone.

Paul and Wendy waited outside. They grew a little anxious after ten minutes passed by.

"Father God," Wendy said out loud, "Thank you for being in control of this situation. Lord, thank you for watching over us and keeping us safe. Thank you that you have called Paul and me to work together like this at this time. Forgive us, Lord, for all that we do that doesn't please you. Please use us to bless Dré and his family. Please save our souls, Lord, and help us to be ready when Jesus comes."

The front door opened and Dré stepped out with a hood pulled up over his head.

"Amen," Paul said. They were both relieved to see him. "What are you wearing, man? You need a shirt and tie."

Dré pulled down the neck of his sweatshirt slightly to show that he was wearing appropriate attire underneath.

They observed the way Dré carried himself as they were walking to the bus stop and concluded that Dré needed to project a tough image as he walked through those streets.

Most of the buildings they passed either needed to be repaired or torn down. The neglected buildings were fertile ground for criminal activity. A youngster like Dré would be easy prey for recruitment. As they boarded the bus, Paul thought about what Ms. Norton said about these youngsters dual identity. The way Dré dressed himself on that morning illustrated that: hoodlum on the outside; gentleman within.

CHAPTER FIFTEEN

Paul adopted Dré as a little brother by spending far more time with him than the internship required. He prayed that he would have a lasting positive impact on the youngster's life. He brought Dré to the college campus to play basketball. On one occasion, he invited him over to watch a game. He took him to the library and started tutoring him in Math. He also talked to Dré about that pivotal moment in American history when the country would elect its first African American president. Paul and his peers felt optimistic that Senator Barack Obama would win.

Some students cut classes on Election Day.

The African and American Students Union went as a group to cast their votes for President of the United States. Crowds had gathered at the polling station, and there was an electricity in the atmosphere that Sergio didn't remember feeling when he'd voted in the presidential elections four years before. Regardless of their race and whether they were voting for the first time, voters sensed that the election marked a defining moment in American history.

The students reconvened outside the building as they waited for everyone from their group to vote. Strangers stopped to talk to one another on the street. Older voters cast the group an admiring glance; some gave them a thumbs-up.

"We're making history," Sergio said.

An elderly gentleman passing near him stopped short.

"What did you say, young man?" he asked Sergio.

The group stopped their conversation and turned their attention to the older gentleman.

"We're making history, Sir. We're electing the first black president of the United States."

"You think he's going to win," the older man stated.

"Yes, Sir."

"Are you sure about that?"

"Yes, Sir."

"I never thought I would ever live to see this day. Look around you. Blacks and whites are coming together to elect a black man for President. And we have you, the younger generation to thank for this."

"No, Sir. We should be thanking you. Your generation sacrificed your lives, so that we could have such a bright future today," Sergio reminded him.

Tears glistened in the old man's eyes, and for a moment, he said nothing. Then, he looked around at the youthful faces in the group. "God bless you. Don't waste the opportunities you've been given. Dream big. Set high goals and persevere until you reach them. Know your history, so you appreciate the present. And live so that the next generation will look up and thank you one day." He sniffled as he walked away.

"Wow!" Monique said, after the gentleman walked away. "That was deep. I don't think I'm going to be able to sleep tonight."

"Let's go to Harlem," Sergio suggested.

"Harlem, New York?" Monique asked.

"Yes. Home of the Apollo Theater and Sylvia's soul food. Home to Congressman Charlie Rangel, and his predecessor Adam Clayton Powell, Jr. Historically, the largest black community in New York, once an underfinanced ghetto; now an upscale part of the city. What else do you want to know?"

"Okay, walking encyclopedia."

"What about the party in the auditorium?" Another student reminded them that the fraternities and sororities had organized across racial lines for the college community to come together to watch the announcement of the election results on television. Constance and Brad would be hosting that event because they both served as student leaders for the college's media. They also produced college based radio and television programs.

"I can't hang with that crowd tonight," Sergio said. "I'm going to Harlem, even if I'm going by myself."

Monique walked over to her boyfriend who was standing with a group of heavyset fellows from the football team. Her number one reason for dating him was that he was a star quarterback with NFL dreams that fit her desire for affluence and recognition. They didn't have much in common and argued often. She feared him when he lost his temper. She loved his body, and the fact that other women were jealous of her because she was with him.

"We should go too, Kane," she suggested sweetly.

"How are you going to get there?" Kane asked Sergio.

"The bus and the train."

"We could drive," Monique offered.

"It's too hard to find parking in the city," Kane said, shaking his head.

Sergio listened to their conversation. He preferred riding his bicycle to local destinations. When he had to travel into Manhattan, he used public transportation because parking spots were scarce and the parking garages charged too much.

"If we go now, while it's so early, we'll find parking." Monique offered that solution. Intellectually, she connected more with Sergio than Kane. She shared Sergio's sentiments about the significance of that moment and the need to be a part of history in the making.

Kane and his teammates insisted on returning to the college campus. As they began to walk back, Kane noticed that Monique wasn't following him.

"Monique, let's go," he commanded.

Monique shook her head. She was standing next to Sergio when she replied, "I want to go to Harlem."

Kane glared at her and Sergio real hard before he walked away.

Sergio missed the look Kane had given him. He was texting Wendy. "I'm Harlem bound," he wrote.

"When?" Wendy asked, replying almost instantly.

"Now."

"Why?"

"Making history. Coming?"

"No."

"Come with us. We're going to wait there for the election results."

"Cool."

"Come with."

"No. Have fun."

"What are you going to do?"

"A group of us is getting together to pray for Senator Barack Obama's safety."

"You are all that."

"JESUS is," Wendy type.

"Later, Holy Roller. LOL." Sergio added the acronym for laugh out loud to show that he was joking. "Pray for me too."

"Always."

Sergio, Monique, and their friends were among thousands of people who flocked to Harlem to wait for the election results. They joined an atmosphere of joyful expectation. Anonymous and famous faces alike held on to hope.

"He's gonna do it," someone shouted.

"Yes, we can. Yes, we can," the crowd chanted.

They felt relieved that they had gotten into the city early. They ate at a local restaurant where the television was tuned to the news and everyone was talking about the election. After they ate, they joined the crowd that was gathering in front of the Harlem State Office Building.

As they watched the big screen television, they saw similar rallies further downtown in Times Square. A group of people who were diverse in race, age, and social class were unified in their expectancy on that night.

Senator Barack Obama secured one state after another, and Monique and Sergio began to dance to the drum roll. The streets of Harlem were alive with the vibrant beat sparked by African drummers. When the television stations officially projected that the African American Senator would become the forty-fourth President of the United States of America, the crowd went wild. People hugged and high-fived, screamed and cried.

Sergio and Monique held each other with tears in their eyes and shared a deep, passionate kiss. Their excitement over the election win nullified any self-consciousness they might have felt otherwise.

"Ain't no stopping us now," blared from the loud speaker as the crowd sang along to the 1979 hit song by McFadden and Whitehead. "We're on the move."

The same song was playing back at the university where Brad and Constance held onto one microphone and sang, "Don't you let nothing, nothing stand in your way. I want you to listen, listen to every word I say. Ain't no stopping us now. We're on the move."

Everyone started dancing the electric slide.

A hush fell on the crowd when the television focused on Grant Park in Chicago, where the new First Family was about to take the stage. Screams of excitement filled the air as incoming President Barack Obama, his wife: First Lady Michelle, and their daughters came into view.

Tears streamed down the faces of famous people like Oprah Winfrey and Jesse Jackson, and tears streamed down the faces Constance and Brad who stood side by side, hand in hand, their own distinctly different racial backgrounds symbolizing the racial unity that had brought about this victory.

Paul drove home earlier that day to wait for the election results with the woman he felt needed him most on that night. During the months leading up to the election, his mother had often reminded him to pray for two people, "Wendy and that fine young man who is running for president."

"Listen to me, Son," Madge Chambers told Paul. "Moving up doesn't have to mean moving away from the people you love most. Take them on the journey with you."

He vividly remembered his mother's tearful story of how her family had marched on Washington with Reverend Dr. Martin Luther King. She told him time and time again how they mourned Dr. King's death, not just as an untimely loss of life, but because it seemed to devalue every black man's life and represented a loss of the civil rights they had strived to gain. She coupled those memories with the fact that her husband—Paul's father—had lost his life in the line of duty as a police officer. And she prayed with Paul that the bright young Senator in his quest for the presidency would not meet the same end.

"Father God, we ask you to put a hedge of protection around the Obama family. Protect them, Lord, from all hurt harm and danger seen and unseen. Let no weapon that is formed against them prosper. Guide them, guard them, and keep them in all their ways, by your grace and mercy, Lord, in Jesus' precious name. Amen."

"Amen," Paul agreed.

As they watched the news that evening, Paul felt satisfied that he had made the right decision to be there with her. His mother didn't need to be alone. She had raised him with an appreciation for the progress African Americans had made, and a consciousness of the painful past they had overcome. He hadn't wanted her to be alone.

When the newscasters announced the election of the first black president of the United States, Madge Chambers collapsed in tears in her son's arms.

"I wish your father had lived to witness this night," she said. After a while, she sniffled and smiled, "I'm glad you came home, Son."

Paul felt tears streaming down his face too. The channel they were watching did a good job of placing the election in historical context, so that even an alien just landing on earth would not have missed the significance of that moment. Yes, the United States had made great strides in its treatment of African Americans, moving away from a past tarnished by slavery. Black people were no longer considered possessions to be listed among the inventory in a slave owner's ledger. One black person counted as a total human being, instead of three-fifths of one as American history had tallied them in the past.

Blacks and whites had paid a high price for progress; many sacrificed their own lives. Yet, in spite of all the progress, children like Dré were at risk of ending up in prison instead of college. Dré and his peers faced the threat of not living to see their twenty-first birthday.

Later that night, when his mother was once again caught up in the jubilation of the moment, Paul dialed Dré's number to find out if he had watched the elections results unfold. He was surprised when Dré's mother said he hadn't been home that evening, and she didn't know where he was. Paul prayed that Dré would stay out of trouble.

As he prayed, Paul's thoughts shifted to Wendy. A quiet evening at home with his mother would have been enough for her on a night like this.

She would share his fulfillment in being there for his mother. He remembered how she used to enjoy going with them to a nursing home to visit their relative. While they were in high school, they had gone almost every week. Wendy didn't need a spotlight to make her feel like she was doing something worthwhile.

Constance, on the other hand, relished the spotlight. She often sacrificed the individual for the crowd. She ranked the college's need for her to DJ an event over Paul's desire to be with his mother on election night.

Paul realized now that in choosing a spouse from between those two women, Wendy complemented him more.

"Paul!" His mother's eyes sparkled and she wore a wide smile.

"Yes, Mom." He wondered what epiphany she had just experienced.

"Don't you see that you and Wendy are like President Obama and his wife First Lady Michelle? Wendy is the one who shares your vision for what you really want to do with your life. She believes in you and will stand by you through the highs and lows of life. Constance is just interested in the spotlight."

Paul nodded, but he wished his mother had praised Wendy without mentioning Constance. "I know, Ma. I'm not going to marry Constance."

"Praise the Lord! You broke off the engagement."

"Not officially. She is still wearing the ring. The ring belonged to her mother who died when she was very young. That's one of the things we have in common, Mom: losing a parent. Constance isn't so bad, if you get to know her. There is a lot to love about her, but I agree that Wendy and I are more compatible."

"Good. So when are you going to break off the engagement?"

"Constance and I have an understanding. You know she is good at recognizing talent and promoting people. She deserves all the credit for my music career."

His mother shrugged.

"Well, she has me booked for performances through next spring, and if I cancel, that will damage her reputation in the entertainment industry. So, I'm going to keep working. The money is pretty good. When she graduates next semester, we'll part ways."

"So she knows you're not planning to marry her?"

"I don't think she wants to marry me, at this point. She says I'm not who she thought I was. But she is very image conscious, so I'll give her time to break up with me."

"In the meantime, what about Wendy?"

"We're back to being friends. She would have been here tonight, if we were together."

"I know that."

Paul smiled. His mother had such confidence in Wendy, and he had to admit, she was right.

"Don't let her go again, Paul."

"I won't, Ma. I love her too much."

"Now that's what I like to hear."

Wendy prayed with the group from the Christian students' fellowship until the television station projected the victory of incoming President Barack Obama. At that point, Wendy returned to her room to call her parents in Jamaica. She didn't get through at first because the circuits were busy.

Instead, she called her family in the Bronx.

Aunt Pat and Uncle Trevor were watching television with their daughter, her husband, and their two children.

"But look what I live to see!" Uncle Trevor exclaimed.

Aunt Pat echoed those sentiments. "Wendy, did you talk to your mother?" she asked.

"Not yet, Aunt Pat. I'm trying to get through."

"You know the whole world is watching and celebrating this great day in American history."

"Yes, Aunt Pat."

After speaking briefly to everyone, Wendy hung up and tried to call her parents again.

"Hello."

"Hi, Daddy."

"Wendy! We were trying to call you."

"I was trying to call you too. Are you watching the election news?"

"Are we? We are the official headquarters. We had a lot of American tourist at the hotel, so we decided to have a party in the banquet hall, so they could watch CNN on the big screen TV. Who knew that even the Prime Minister of Jamaica would join us?"

"God." Wendy giggled. So her parents were hobnobbing with the island's most prominent politician.

"Yes, God knew. You're right. What are you doing? I imagine there are college parties going on."

"Yes, but I'm in my room."

"Alone. Why?"

"That's where I want to be."

"I hope you're not there sulking over Paul Chambers."

"No, Dad."

"Wendy?"

"Daddy, I promise you, I'm not here sulking over Paul. Paul and I have been getting along well."

"Good. So is he there with you?"

"No. Where is Mommy?"

Devon decided not to question his daughter further, especially because his wife was beside him anxiously waiting for the phone. "She's right here. I love you."

"I love you too, Daddy."

"Hold on for your mother."

"Hey, baby-girl. Is this night going down in history for this momentous election, as well as the night you and Paul got back together?"

"No, Mommy. Paul and I are not back together, but we're good friends again." Wendy spoke quickly to try to shift the focus back to the reason for her call. "America has a black president, Mommy. Can you believe it?"

"My dear! If you see the celebration going on down here, you would think it was a Jamaican election and not in the States."

"Well, what happens in the United States affects the world."

"You've got that right!"

If Wendy could have seen her parents at that moment they were holding hands and staring into each other's eyes, as though they were the only ones present in the crowded ballroom.

"Wendy, your father and I have some more news."

"You're having a baby."

"Yes!"

Wendy screamed. "Oh my goodness! I don't believe you. I was only kidding." She giggled.

"Well, we're not. You're going to have a little brother or sister."

"Marcia and Devon Douglas, aren't you a little old for that?" Wendy joked.

Marcia held the phone so Devon could hear their daughter's reaction.

"Hey now, Missy," Devon chided, but his voice resonated humor.

"I'm only kidding. Congratulations!" A pause and then, "Wow! Only God."

"Praise the Lord! Hallelujah! Thank you, Jesus!"

"Ya'll keep praising Him now."

Her parents laughed. "We love you!"

"I love you too."

Wendy hung up the phone and cried. Her emotions peaked in tears of joy at the outcome of the election, and at the news from her parents. She praised God for the miracle of her parents' love. Wendy's parents had been teenage lovers. Her father hadn't been around when Wendy was born. Her mother had lied to him and told him that the baby she was expecting wasn't his because he would have insisted that she have an abortion. Her mother was brave enough to keep the baby, but succumbed to a bout of depression that might have ended in suicide if her Aunt Pat hadn't intervened. Aunt

Pat had brought Wendy and her mother from their home in Jamaica to her home in New York where Wendy grew up.

"Only God," Wendy said out loud.

She remembered how her mother struggled to forgive her father and accept his overtures of love, at first. Wendy and Paul covered them with their prayers, and eventually, God replaced all bitterness and regret with forgiveness and reconciliation.

Wendy longed to talk to Paul at that moment. In spite of their two-year separation, he still knew her best. She wouldn't have to explain to him how she felt. He would understand. But she wouldn't allow herself to rely on him while he was still engaged to marry Constance Channing.

CHAPTER SIXTEEN

A buzz of excitement emanated from the group gathered in Professor Abbey's class on the day after the election. If anyone felt disappointed about the election results, they didn't express their feelings. Everyone seemed happy, excited, and optimistic about the future.

"I need you all to settle down," Professor Abbey directed the group. "We still have to get some work done."

"Awe," they groaned.

Professor Abbey continued: "During the semester, we have discussed how crime, poverty, and substance abuse have obscured the American Dream for some blacks in America. We see particular problems in the neighboring city where so many youth have lost their lives to violent crime. For some politicians, like Mayor Corey Booker in Newark, the issue is paramount. Yet, the issue was absent from the presidential platform leading up to the election. What impact do you think the election of a black president will have on our youth, particularly those in communities plagued with violent crime?"

Monique raised her hand. "I have no doubt that our youth will be inspired by a black president. At the community center where I work, the youngsters I spoke with watched the debates, and they were all impressed by President Obama's oratory skills. That sounds good doesn't it? We have a black president!" She grinned, and stood up and hooted before she continued, "I'm sorry. I'm just so happy. And that's how the kids are. They're happy too, and excited, and they want to do good things. Great things. You know?"

Professor Abbey chuckled. He too shared their excitement and a sense of personal pride. After all, the incoming president's father hailed from Kenya, thereby making him a son of Africa to Professor Abbey. He too brimmed with emotion filled with expectation that America's highest office was attainable to an immigrant family—to a first generation American.

"Is that the consensus? That we're all big dreamers with great aspirations driven toward success, inspired by this moment in history."

Paul raised his hand.

Professor Abbey nodded in acknowledgement.

"I agree with Monique, in part, but there is evidence that some youth are still falling through the cracks. For example, Wendy and I work with a client who lives in dire poverty. The building he lives in looks abandoned. The staircase seems like at any moment it could collapse. His mother is a drug-addict who keeps having children but doesn't stay sober long enough to take care of them. He is already caught up in the criminal justice system. I tried to engage him in paying attention to the elections, but he couldn't see what that was going to do for him. He could see the immediate benefit of going to work for the drug dealer up the street, but he could not see how the president's office would affect his life."

"Do you agree with Paul's assessment, Wendy?"

"Yes, Professor Abbey. I mean, we pray for this kid all the time. He is smart and polite once you get past the tough front he puts up. But when you go by his home and see how his family lives, and when you walk the streets of his neighborhood, it just seems like he's doomed."

"I don't think there is any doom and gloom in America at this moment," Monique interjected. "This is what the generations before us died for."

"True But Monique, you have to admit that some youngsters today are dying for nothing. Reverend Dr. Martin Luther King, and the freedom riders, and those who laid down their lives to get us the right to attend colleges like this one, died for a cause. Kids today are dying because someone looked at them the wrong way, or messed with their girlfriend, or infringed on their turf. It's almost like they don't value their own lives." The student who spoke was seated beside Monique.

Monique turned to face him directly. "Some. Some youngsters are like that, but most are bright and ambitious. And thanks to President Obama, they can now see that they can be anything they want to be." She started singing and bopping, "Ain't no stopping us now; we're on the move…"

Some of the other students joined her in singing. The student on the other side of her slapped her a high five.

"This is still a class," Professor Abbey reminded them. "Let's maintain an atmosphere that promotes scholarship. You'll have plenty of opportunities outside of this room for celebration."

Wendy and Paul looked at each other. They could argue further by citing specifics about Dré, but Ms. Torrell had drilled into them the need for confidentiality. They also prayed that Monique was right, and that the election of a black president would change things for the better for every child in every community.

"Here is your assignment," Professor Abbey continued, handing them a sheet of paper with guidelines. "Write a five to ten-page paper about the impact of last night's election. Focus on the election results, the significance thereof, and the jubilation that it has generated worldwide. While generalizations and symbolism are important, I want you to cite specific details. You may make predictions, using evidence you uncover in today's society, and four years from now, you may want to re-read these papers and see if your foresight was accurate. The paper is due at the start of our first class next week. Any questions?"

Student shook their heads. No one said anything.

"Very well then. Start your papers immediately. E-mail me any questions you have, and I'll respond to you promptly. I will not be responding to questions during the last forty-eight hours before class. By then, you should have completed your initial draft and be revising it."

"This is too much. I need more time," one student complained. "I can't…"

"Yes, you can," Professor Abbey corrected her. "All together now, 'Yes, we can. Yes, we can.'"

The slogan from President Obama's campaign rekindled the excitement that had stirred up the students from the beginning of the class. Students left the room discussing the election results and their optimism about the future.

"Wendy, wait up," Paul called out as they were leaving the room.

She had rushed out of the room, hoping to meet Sergio before he headed back to his apartment. She stepped to the side of the hallway and waited for Paul to catch up to her.

"Hi." He grasped both of her hands and made eye contact.

"What's up?"

He smiled at her, feeling warmed by her closeness. "My mom says hi."

"You were with her last night." Wendy's comment was a more of a statement than a question. "I figured as much. How is she?"

"Ecstatic, like everyone else. What an emotional night, huh?"

"For real!"

"What did you do?"

"Pray and watch TV."

"With Sergio?" Paul asked, suddenly feeling jealous and surprised at himself. Sergio's popularity and Wendy's unpopularity made them a prominent and odd pair. Coming to terms with his feelings for Wendy the night before made Paul desire to be the one she was confiding in.

"Sergio Rayford? Uh uh. Prayer is not his cup of tea. I was with the group from Christian Fellowship. After our prayer meeting, I went back to my room.'"

"Oh." Paul felt relieved, but longed for them to be together.

Wendy removed her hands from his grasp and started walking toward the exit.

Paul kept pace with her. "Have you spoken to our friend?" he asked. Following Ms. Torrell's rules regarding confidentiality, they didn't refer to Dré by name.

"No. We need to call him to remind of his appointment tomorrow morning."

"I've been calling him since yesterday. No luck. I pray he's alright."

Wendy heard the worry in Paul's voice and looked over at him. "He's probably fine. Just hanging out, maybe."

"That's what got him in trouble in the first place. I've been praying that he would really turn his life around."

"Me too. You've spent a lot of time with him."

"Small thing, really. He's like the little brother I never had."

"Speaking of little brothers, you'll never guess what I just found out." Wendy stopped and turned to Paul, her eyes sparkling with excitement.

They had just stepped outside the building and Paul had noticed both Constance and Sergio socializing with different groups along the pathway. He turned his attention to Wendy, pleased that she wasn't running away, or avoiding him, but was sharing her excitement with him in front of everyone. "Your Aunt Blossom's having another baby."

"Wrong. My parents are having a baby."

"What? Pops is no joke." He covered his mouth with his right hand. "What? Wow!"

Wendy giggled. "I know. At first, I was like, 'You guys are too old.' And then I realized, not really, because they were so young when they had me, you know. So I'm going to be old enough to be my baby brother or sister's mother. Life is funny."

"God has a sense of humor. You seem really happy though." He felt the urge to reach out and stroke her cheek, but he didn't.

"I'm so happy for them. It's amazing to see how God is working in their lives since they surrendered everything to him. I mean they've been through so much. Who would have thought their latter days would be their better days?"

"God."

"They love each other so much. Now Daddy is pampering Mommy and doing all the things he didn't do when she was pregnant with me."

His eyes searched hers for any sadness, but instead he saw sincere joy. His heart screamed, "I love you, Wendy Tapper Douglas," but he couldn't say it just yet. Instead, he said, "I'm happy that you're so happy."

She smiled at him, grateful for the friendship she was feeling between them. No one else would understand the full significance of the news about her parents. She and Paul had a history together that made their compassion for each other run deep.

"Tell Pops I said congratulations," Paul requested.

"Tell him yourself. You should call them. They'd be so happy to hear from you."

Again, Paul's eyes searched hers and saw nothing but sincere warmth and acceptance. He pulled out his cell phone. "What's their number?"

She told him. Then they agreed on what time and where they would meet the next morning to pick up Dré and escort him to court.

As Wendy and Paul parted ways, Sergio walked away from the group he was standing with and came over to meet her. They followed the pathway toward the campus parking lot.

"What's up with you and Romeo Singer over there?"

"Nothing."

"Nothing," he mimicked her. "You are so smitten. It's not even funny. Don't let him break your heart again."

"He won't," Wendy replied quickly and confidently.

Sergio frowned at her, but he offered no comment.

"So what are we having for lunch?" Wendy asked.

"We were out all night last night celebrating. Wendy Douglas, we are living in a changed world. Yesterday, I didn't think I could be a future president of the United States. Today, I know I can."

Wendy smiled at him as he unlocked his bicycle from the stand by the parking lot. "I can see it now." She held up her hands with her palms facing Sergio and read the imaginary headline: "From college president to US president; Sergio Rayford's road to the White House."

"Not really. But it's so good to see a black man shatter that glass ceiling. President Barack Obama. I love it! A black president in the White House. He just burst that barrier wide open. Now the sky really is the limit."

They walked the distance to his apartment. Sergio rolled his bicycle alongside them as they traveled, talking about the events of the night before.

As he unlocked the door to his apartment, he marveled at the outcome of the presidential elections and declared, "Yes, there is a God."

"Yes, there is. Do you have any idea how many prayers have been said for the Obamas?" Wendy asked.

"I know. Now, everyone is praying for his safety," Sergio observed.

"He'll be alright."

"You think so?"

"God didn't bring him this far to leave him."

Sergio didn't feel the confidence Wendy displayed. Her faith in God seemed to give her a peace of mind that he didn't have.

"Black men lose their lives every day for little or nothing, and the world doesn't care, but if anything happened to this black man..." Sergio didn't dare state the consequences, as though speaking it would increase its likelihood of happening.

Wendy placed her hand over his. "Would you indulge me for a minute?"

Sergio looked down at her and shrugged.

"Let's pray." Wendy didn't wait for him to object. She held both his hands and closed her eyes. "Father God, we thank you that you are and that through Jesus we have life and that more abundantly. Father, we thank you for the life that you have given us that has brought us to this day. We pray that you place a hedge of protection around President Barack Obama, Lord. Guard him and his wife First Lady Michelle. Protect their daughters, Lord, and their grandmother. Guard and protect the Vice President and his family, and all those who support the Obamas, Lord. Let no weapons formed against them prosper, and condemn every tongue that rises against them in judgment. We love you, Lord. We thank you for this day. We ask that you forgive us of our sins and prepare our hearts so that we will be ready when Jesus comes. In Jesus' name, we pray ask and give you the glory. Amen."

Sergio's voice was husky when he said, "Amen." As Wendy prayed, he felt something. It was an unfamiliar feeling, but he was deeply moved. He couldn't explain it, except to agree that there was power in prayer. He opened his eyes and saw Wendy looking at him with tenderness in her eyes.

"Admit it. You love me," he said.

Wendy laughed. "Of course I do. You are my brother."

"Yeah, yeah, yeah. You know how many women out there are dying to get a piece of this," Sergio said, flexing his muscles, "Here you have me all to yourself, and you let it go to waste."

Wendy walked into the kitchen. "So, brother, what are you making for lunch?"

A lewd answer popped into his mind, but he respected Wendy too much to say it. He washed his hands and got busy preparing the meal. "Will you make us something to drink?" he asked. "Use the juicer. It's right next to the bowl of fruit."

Wendy and Sergio had just finished eating and were getting ready to clean up when he shared a text message he'd just received with her.

"Monique wants me to take her to the Apollo Theater. She won tickets from a radio show."

"Cool. But why isn't she going with her boyfriend?"

"She said he has a game. Do you think I should go?"

"I don't know. Her boyfriend is really possessive. Did he go to Harlem with you guys last night?"

"No. He didn't seem too happy about Monique going either, but she didn't care. I'm glad she went with us. You should have been there too. I don't know how to describe it to you. It was an amazing night."

"Two nights in Harlem with a woman who's committed to another man. I don't know, Sergio. You're asking for trouble."

"And you're not? The man you're over here daydreaming about marrying is engaged to someone else."

"It's not the same thing."

"No. Your situation is worse than mine. I'm not trying to get with Monique. We're just friends."

"Yeah, but with your reputation, her boyfriend is bound to think something's going on between you two."

"I'll let her deal with that. A concert at the Apollo, just two nights after the election. That's just too good to pass up." He typed in three letters and pressed the send button.

Wendy realized he'd responded, "Yes."

"I'll be praying for you, my brother."

"You do that."

"Jesus loves you, and so do I."

CHAPTER SEVENTEEN

Paul and Wendy parked their cars near the law office and took the bus over to the block where Dré lived. The sun-filled blue sky contrasted sharply with the gloominess on that street. The buildings looked burnt-out, decayed and abandoned. Each lump of clothing bundled near a vent or grate next to a building turned out to be a homeless person huddled in a corner sleeping on the sidewalk seeking warmth. The ground floor of two buildings stood out as being well maintained: the corner store and a restaurant that sold fried chicken. Chicken bones and non-biodegradable containers littered the sidewalk.

Paul placed his hand in the hole where a lock should have been and opened the door to Dré's building. He entered the dark foyer and called out Dré's name. Dré had become accustomed to them picking him up and usually responded quickly, fully dressed and ready to leave. This time Paul heard no answer.

"Dré," Paul called out more loudly this time.

Wendy stood behind him holding her cell phone in her hand. "I'll call him," she said.

Paul nodded.

The phone rang until the call disconnected because no one picked up.

"You wait down here. I'm going upstairs."

On all their previous visits, they had never climbed the stairs. Wide cracks weakened the foundations, and the banister was broken and provided no support. In spite of that, Dré usually sped up and down the stairs like he had wings.

As Paul slowly and carefully climbed the stairs, Wendy remembered the first time they met Dré at that building.

"Why didn't you come upstairs?" he asked, when he came out to meet them. "What's the matter; you scared?"

Truth be told, Wendy had felt afraid, but when she looked at Dré's face, she saw innocence there. His innocent look belied the violent acts the prosecutor accused him of committing.

"Self defense, peer pressure, a product of his environment…" Those were the arguments the public defender presented in his favor. It would take a miracle to transform Dré's life, to redirect him from following his father's footsteps to long-term incarceration or his mother's path to senseless substance abuse. Paul and Wendy prayed for that miracle, and Paul had tried to stay in touch with Dré, spending far more time with him than he needed to, hoping to be that positive influence in bettering Dré's life.

Paul knocked on the door upstairs. He knocked louder each time until someone finally answered.

"Who is it? What do you want?"

Wendy heard a woman's voice resonate with annoyance.

Paul politely introduced himself—again. He'd met Dré's mother more than once when he'd picked up Dré on the weekend to take him to play basketball, to the library, or to visit the college. Dré told him his mother wouldn't remember.

"She's stoned, man. She don't remember nothing no more." Dré had tried to laugh off his mother's incoherence, but sadness clouded his eyes.

Paul felt the weight of that sadness personally as he faced Dré's mother.

Dré's mother took one look at Paul and squealed. "I ain't got none. I ain't giving it up," she cried and retreated back inside the room.

Paul caught the door as she attempted to slam it and shouted to Wendy to come on up. He quickly surmised that Dré's mother was hallucinating, or perhaps she thought he was a pimp or a pusher looking for a prostitute. Dré had told him some candid stories about the life she lived in front of her children. Those stories made Paul wish he had a home of his own already and could adopt Dré and give him a permanent safe place to live, although Dré's concern for his younger siblings was so great, he might not have wanted to leave. To them, the place seemed uninhabitable; to Dré, this was home.

"Ma'am, please don't be afraid of us," Wendy entreated softly. "You've met us before. Remember? We usually pick up your son Dré for his appointments. He is a supposed to be in court this morning. Can you tell us where he is?"

"I ain't seen him."

"Did he leave for school this morning?"

"Dré goes to school all day. He… he never miss a class. He is a good kid. He 'posed to take the baby to the sitter. You see Dré? Dré. Dré." She yelled her son's name at the top of her lungs.

In response to her yelling, a baby started crying. Paul and Wendy turned to see Dré's baby brother on a bare mattress that was lying on the floor, surrounded by dirty clothes and other items.

"Dré? Where you been boy? Got this lady up here looking for you, getting all up in my space. At least you ready to go. Now get!"

Wendy turned and Paul spun around completely to see if Dré had indeed entered the room. It took them a moment to realize that Dré's mother was talking to Paul, who was still standing near the doorway of the dimly lit room.

"Ma'am. That's not your son," Wendy informed her.

"What do you mean that's not my son?"

"That's Paul Chambers. He and I came here to pick up Dré and take him to court."

"So take him then. Take him. And get up out a here before I have you arrested for trespassing."

Paul and Wendy looked at each other, stumped at what to do.

"I said get. Leave. You see the door; now get to steppin'."

Paul and Wendy stood frozen in place, shocked by the erratic behavior of Dré's mother.

"I said get out!" she yelled, staggering toward Paul. "Don't let me have to call the police."

Wendy bypassed her and followed Paul out the door.

"If you see Dré, tell him to bring me back my money." She laughed hysterically as she slammed the door shut and locked it.

Paul and Wendy didn't speak to each other until they made their way down the stairs and outside of the building.

"Oh my goodness!" Wendy spoke in a raspy voice.

Paul looked at her and saw tears in her eyes. He held her hand and tugged her gently, so they would keep walking up the block. "It's going to be alright. Have faith in God."

"I do, but what are we going to do? We can't just leave that baby in there. That can't be safe."

"I'm going to call the office. You call Ms. Torrell on her cell phone."

They walked briskly, remaining alert, subtly watching their backs, but trying not to look paranoid. Dressed in their business suits and trench coats, they stood out on those streets, labeled by the residents as social workers.

Paul spoke to someone in the law office, but Wendy was unable to reach Ms. Torrell.

"Someone from the office is going to ask child welfare services to send out an investigator," Paul whispered. No one was standing near them, but he still felt the need to be cautious. "What did Ms. Torrell say?"

"I didn't get her. Maybe we should just take the bus down to the courthouse."

"Go ahead. That's what the office wants us to do. I'm going to stay here and try to find Dré."

"I don't think you should."

"I have to."

Wendy understood that Paul cared about Dré, and had bonded with him to a point that would outlast their internship experience. She could see the bus coming down the street.

"Where will you go?" she asked.

"By his school, the police precinct, the basketball court… This is the first time he hasn't been ready and waiting for us. Something's wrong."

"Be careful, Paul. It's life and death in these streets."

"I know, but my life is worth no more than Dré's."

Wendy's eyes filled up with tears. Her love for Paul never felt stronger than it did at that moment.

"It's going to be alright, Wendy. I'll call you with an update."

Wendy queued up behind a couple of other people who were starting to board the bus.

"I'll be praying for you," she told Paul.

Paul couldn't hold back anymore. "I love you, Wendy, more than I've ever loved anyone in my whole entire life."

Wendy gasped.

Paul kissed her lightly on the lips and gently shoved her toward the bus.

"I love you too," she said before boarding.

"Go ahead, girl!" The bus driver grinned at Wendy as she paid her bus fare. "Each time ya'll get on this bus, I could see the love. Where your man's little brother at today?"

Although they caught the same bus each time, either taking Dré to court, to see his probation officer, or to some other appointment, Wendy was surprised that the bus driver had been paying so much attention to them.

"He's somewhere around," Wendy replied sitting down in front. She felt a little self conscious and wondered if any of the other passengers were regulars and had also been noticing them. She didn't make eye contact with anyone.

As the bus drove off and overtook Paul walking down the street, Wendy stared out the window at him.

He waved.

"Now that seems like a good man right there," the bus driver said.

Wendy smiled and tried to hold back tears. In the midst of their concern over Dré's whereabouts, and despite being shook up by the behavior of Dré's mother and the sight of the baby who seemed to be in danger, the cloud that seemed to be hanging over them had a silver lining. Paul had declared his love for her for the first time in two and a half years. She prayed that God would keep him safe, and that by the time she reached the courthouse, he would have already found Dré.

The day didn't unfold with the results Wendy had been praying for. She met Ms. Torrell in court where they explained to the judge about Dré's living condition and about how his mother may have forced him to run an errand without realizing how essential it was for him to show up for his court date.

The prosecutor asked the judge to issue a warrant for Dré's arrest. Ms. Torrell argued that given his consistent accountability prior to this date, they should reschedule the court appearance. The judge agreed on the condition that the public defender return to court with a recommendation of a permanent residential facility where Dré would be placed.

Wendy left Ms. Torrell at the courthouse attending to her other clients. She dialed Paul's cell phone number.

"Hey."

"How's it going?" she asked him.

"I haven't found him yet. He wasn't at school or at any of his usual hangouts. I'm heading over to the police precinct. Could you call the office and ask them about filing a missing person's report?"

"I think Ms. Torrell would want to be the one to make that decision."

"You're right. Look, I'll call you back."

There was nothing more for Wendy to do but pray. She rode the bus back to the law office and picked up her car from the parking lot. She prayed that God would keep Paul safe and that he would quickly be reunited with Dré.

She parked her car on the college campus and was on her way back to the dorm when she ran into Constance, who was walking with a group of her sorority sisters. Sporting a weave or wig that stopped in the center of her back, shadowed eyes, lipstick and heels, Constance looked glamorous. She always appeared ready for the runway.

As they came alongside each other, Constance declared, "I broke up with Paul You're welcome to the sloppy seconds." The girls who were with her burst out laughing, aiming their derision at Wendy.

Wendy knitted her brows at them but kept walking. The events of that morning heavily outweighed her concern about personal humiliation. Back at the dorm, she took a shower and changed into casual clothes. She wanted to call Paul again, but realized that calling frequently might hamper his efforts, so she decided to wait for him to call with an update.

She picked up her Bible and tried to think of a fitting Scripture to read. She opened it to Psalm 139. The verses she read reassured her that God knew all about her before she was even born. No matter where she went or what she did, she couldn't escape God's presence. He was always there to lead her and guide her through the highs and lows of life. "For you have possessed my reigns; you covered me in my mother's womb." Verse thirteen reminded her that even as she sought to cover Paul with prayer, God had him covered from the moment he was conceived. She prayed that God would continue cover and protect Paul and that soon she would hear that he had found Dré.

She got on her knees and recited the twenty-third Psalm.

"The Lord is my shepherd; I shall not want. He maketh me to lie down in green pastures: he leadeth me beside the still waters. He restoreth my soul: he leadeth me in the paths of righteousness for his name sake. Yea, though I walk through the valley of the shadow of death, I will fear no evil: for thou art with me; thy rod and thy staff they comfort me. Thou preparest a table before me in the presence of mine enemies: thou anointest my head with oil; my cup runneth over. Surely goodness and mercy shall follow me all the days of my life: and I will dwell in the house of the Lord forever."

Late that evening, Paul called her and asked her to come out to the parking lot and meet him at his car. He didn't say anything as he opened the door for her to get in the car beside him.

She sensed his mood and waited for him to speak.

He started the car and drove off campus.

She didn't ask him where they were going. The atmosphere felt weighty and she could tell that Paul was sad.

Eventually, he parked.

She realized that he had found the privacy he was seeking. While they were in high school, they had shared many confidential moments alone in his mother's car.

He shut the car off, but kept his head straight, staring at the windshield.

Wendy pulled her seatbelt and turned to look at him, but waited for him to speak.

Paul maintained his posture, but a tear slid from his eye.

Wendy reached out and wrapped an arm around his neck, her thumb stroking the back of his head. "It's going to be alright, remember?" Unsure of the reason for his sadness, she tried to reassure him with the same words he had spoken to her earlier that day. "Have faith in God."

Paul sobbed outright and turned to look at her.

In all their lives growing up together, Wendy had never seen him cry like this. She wanted to cry too, but resolved to be strong for him.

"Dré... Dré's gone, Wendy," Paul croaked. His voice was extremely hoarse and he could barely say the words. He sobbed hard.

She dared not ask where had Dré gone. She thought she understood what Paul meant, but she refused to believe it. She had prayed too hard, and this was not the outcome she was believing God for.

Paul cried out loud. Anguish racked his body.

She knew for sure now that he meant Dré was gone forever. Silent tears streamed down her face.

After a while Paul inhaled deeply and tried to give her more details. "Ms. Torrell and I ID'd his body." He closed his eyes, trying to block out the image of Dré's lifeless body: so youthful in his face, not fully grown yet, dependent on a parent who couldn't take care of him. He hadn't yet begun to live his life.

Paul couldn't do it. He had maintained his composure as he stood with Ms. Torrell. As he saw her safely back to her car, neither one of them had cried. Ms. Torrell successfully maintained the professional detachment that enabled her to continue to champion the cause of the youngest who lived their lives at risk of getting caught up in violent crime, at risk of being locked up in prison, and at risk of dying before they had even begun to live their adult lives. She had seen this before and chances were she would see it again, and she was determined not to let it break her.

It broke Paul. He had prayed and hoped that Dré would turn his life around, and permanently escape the snares that threatened to destroy him. He couldn't, probably wouldn't, ever understand why Dré had to die.

Wendy prayed that God would give her some words to comfort and strengthen her best friend. She thanked God that she hadn't lost him that way, and she promised herself that they had already wasted enough time. No one knew how much life they had, she thought; no one knew when Jesus was coming, or when they were going. Life was too precious and too short. She started to recite the twenty-third psalm.

Paul sniffled. He looked into Wendy's eyes and saw faith there; faith that rekindled and strengthened his own. It had always been like this between them. He was reminded that he didn't need to search to find the woman who would complete him. She was and had always been right there in front of him. He kissed her now, deeply and passionately, drawing strength from their love.

CHAPTER EIGHTEEN

The concert at the Apollo Theater in Harlem had been planned long before election night to celebrate the anniversary of the first black radio disc jockey, but the cause for celebration turned out to be two-fold.

"For once in my life, I can proudly say, I am a citizen of the United States," joked the celebrity host, but there was a serious message behind his jest. African Americans had long fought for their country in the armed forces. Yet, blacks were often accused of being unpatriotic. Some were apathetic or didn't participate in the political process because up until that presidential election, they still felt disenfranchised, feeling that they were not granted equal opportunities to achieve. "I've been walking around with a big grin on my face, just happy. I can't wipe this smile off since election night."

The seats Monique had won placed her and Sergio in the front row of the balcony, where they had easy viewing of the honoree and all the celebrity artists who came to perform. Some of the artists were old school. Others performed contemporary hits and even gospel songs. Each thanked the radio deejay for playing their music on the air when no one else would. Each one also celebrated the election of the first African American President of the United States.

Sergio and Monique danced in the stands. During the love songs, Sergio wrapped his arm around Monique.

Monique smiled up at him and felt glad that her boyfriend had not come. Sergio shared her appreciation of black history and a mutual excitement about the significance of this moment.

Sergio kissed her.

Monique responded by kissing him back, deciding that on that night Sergio understood her better than anyone else in the world.

By the end of the show, a big screen had been lowered with a picture of the new First Family that was taken on the election night when they all came on stage at Grant Park in Chicago. Dressed in red and black, they appeared to be a model family.

Sergio felt proud just to look at them. He had never had a real family, bouncing from one foster home to another. He wondered what it would have been like to belong to that type of family, with a father who provided for his wife and children and a mother who put the welfare of her children first.

Constance Channing was also sitting in the audience at the Apollo Theater that night. Her father's company owned the radio station that hosted the show, and she had used his name to secure seats for her and two of her sorority sisters. As she viewed the picture of President Barack Obama and his family, she also found herself longing for a father who put his family first. Her father had done a great job of providing things for her, but he was never there. The time she spent with him added up to less than a week each year. One of her sorority sisters pointed out Monique and Sergio kissing in the stands. They thought it was a spicy observation for the gossip mill back at the college, but in that moment, Constance couldn't care less.

After the show, Monique went back to Sergio's apartment. They made love that night, savoring each other and all that was right with the world from their perspective. They hadn't planned this rendezvous that they would now have to keep secret, but it seemed a fitting ending to their night.

Sergio's reputation as a player did little to keep women from falling for him. His handsome face and taut body made him physically appealing, but women loved him even more because he cooked, cleaned and kept his home so comfortable that those who slept over often wanted to move in. After years of maintaining immunity to his charm, Monique found herself falling completely in love with him.

As college students packed up to go home for the Thanksgiving Holiday, she contemplated breaking up with Kane. She and Kane had been in a passionate and volatile relationship for two semesters. Over the summer, they had taken a break from each other and had seen other people, but they had gotten serious again, practically living together since they returned to college that semester. They shared an intense physical attraction, but beyond that they had little in common. She went to many of his games and although football bored her, she loved the idea of becoming a professional athlete's wife.

She and Sergio were getting ready to leave the African and American Students Union office one evening when she asked, "Are you going home for Thanksgiving?"

"I'm already home."

"Seriously."

Sergio shrugged, and picked up his backpack to leave the office.

Monique had replaced him as president of that student organization, and he would serve as president of the student government up until his graduation that summer.

"Are you having Thanksgiving Dinner alone?" Monique asked as she locked up the office.

Sergio stood in the hallway behind her holding her stuff. He nodded in greeting to some other students who were leaving. The building would close soon, and a security officer would patrol to make sure that all the students had indeed gone out.

"Not really," Sergio replied. "I cook a big dinner for everyone who has nowhere else to go. You'd be surprised to see how many people actually hang around here for Thanksgiving."

Monique turned to face him, her eyes filled with admiration. "I had no idea. I just assumed that everyone went home."

"International students and some of the people who make their permanent homes off campus, I never know how many people are going to show up. Some just come for the good food."

"Your cooking is good. Save me some."

"I'll see."

They walked out of the building together. Kane was waiting for Monique outside.

"What's up, man?" Sergio greeted him.

Kane glared at him.

Sergio turned to Monique and handed her all her stuff.

She smiled at him and thanked him.

"Later," Sergio said in parting and walked away.

"You trying to play me, Monique," Kane demanded.

"What do you mean?"

"What's up with you and Sergio? I see the way you look at him."

"Sergio and I are just friends," but even as she said those words, she felt a little dreamy, longing for something more.

"I got a call from a scout from the NFL today."

"You did?"

"Check this out."

Kane handed Monique a newspaper article that touted him as a favorite among NFL draft picks. The amount of money the article mentioned that players got signed for pushed all thoughts of Sergio from her mind.

"Wow, baby! This is great!" She kissed him.

Kane gave her a knowing nod. He knew what made her tick, but he wasn't about to let her use him. When they were alone, he had every intention of showing her who was in charge.

When Sergio got back to his apartment, he was surprised to find Wendy in the lobby waiting for him.

"Couldn't stay away from me, huh?"

She laughed. "Don't be so full of yourself. I just wanted to give you a hug before Paul and I leave for the holiday."

Sergio made a funny face at her. "Paul and I. I tell you, he's one lucky fellow." He embraced Wendy.

"It's a two-way blessing."

"Yeah, okay. Are you coming up?" Sergio gestured toward the stairs.

"No Paul is waiting for me. I told him I wanted to see you before I leave."

"Why are you guys heading out so early?"

"My classes are canceled for tomorrow, and I handed in all my papers. My parents are coming in from Jamaica. I can't wait to see them."

"Happy family reunion," Sergio said, feeling a sense of loss for himself having never had that type of family.

"You could come with us."

"No thank you. Home is where my heart is and my heart is right here."

"Happy Thanksgiving." Wendy kissed him on the cheek.

"To you too, Miss Wendy."

"I'll be praying for you."

"Thank you. I'll be praying for you too."

Their eyes locked and held for a moment, as Wendy appreciated the change she saw in him. Sergio's response to her assurance that she would be praying for him used to be, "You do that." She marveled at how God had used Dré's death to draw Sergio closer to him. Sergio remembered Dré well from his visits with Paul at the college. He had played basketball with them in the gym a few times, and had seen them reading in the library.

"I give Paul props for really trying to make a difference in his life. How is he taking it?" Sergio had asked Wendy when she told him what had happened to Dré.

"Hard." Wendy's curt response reflected the sadness she also felt.

"I'm really sorry." Sergio hadn't told anyone, but he saw a lot of himself in Dré. He related to Dré because he too had had a no-show father and a mother whose life was consumed by substance abuse. After years of listening to Wendy but not hearing her, he suddenly realized that but for the grace of God that could have been him. "Let me know the funeral arrangements. I'll be there."

Sergio meant what he said and had stood beside Paul and Wendy as they said their last goodbye to Dré. When it was over, he shook Paul's hand and gave him a man-hug: that quick embrace and pound on the back. And that night, Sergio prayed for himself, for his mother and for Dré's mother.

He wasn't sure he was doing it right, but he just talked to the Lord. He asked God to forgive him and to help him forgive his mother. He asked God to save his mother and Dré's and to deliver them from the vices that had consumed their lives. He found the Bible that Wendy had given him and he looked up the Scripture the preacher had read at Dré's funeral.

In Matthew, chapter eighteen, in the tenth verse, Sergio read, "Take heed that you despise not one of these little ones: for I say unto you, that in heaven their angels do always behold the face of my Father which is in heaven." He had no prior knowledge that the Bible said that. In that verse, Sergio felt like Jesus was telling him that when children were forced or led into sin by the adults around them, and they died in that sin, that God had a place in heaven for each and every one of those children. He found comfort in that, and for the first time in his own life, he felt like he just might find a father in God.

He never explained how he felt to Wendy, but she noticed a change in the way he responded to her each time she mentioned that she was praying for him, and she praised God.

Sergio watched as she walked away.

Wendy turned to wave to him one last time before exiting through the front door.

Wendy and Paul pulled up in separate cars in front of his mother's home. It was dark outside and the block was pretty quiet. Paul swung his weekend bag over his shoulder and locked up his car. He turned to Wendy and held out his hand. His heart soared as he felt her touch.

A feeling of nostalgia overwhelmed Wendy. During high school, Paul's house had been her home away from home. She felt most thankful that they were together again and wondered how they could have ever been apart. Everything felt right about their relationship. Always had, and she prayed that from that point forward, it always would.

Paul unlocked the door and placed a finger against his lips reminding Wendy to be quiet.

"Paul, honey, is that you?" his mother called out. She entered the living room and squealed when she saw Wendy standing there with him. "Oh… oh…" Madge Chambers found herself at a loss for words. Then she threw her hands up in the air and said, "Thank you, Jesus! Come here, my children." She wrapped them both in a tight embrace.

Wendy spent the next couple hours with Paul and his mother.

His mother fed them and fussed over them. She didn't ask for details about their reconciliation, nor did she ask what happened to Constance. She felt effused with joy just to see Paul and Wendy together again. This was a direct answer to her prayers and she continued to praise the Lord.

"Mrs. Chambers, when was the last time you spoke to my mom?"

"Oh! She called me the other day to tell me that she and your father are expecting a baby. I'm so happy for her. God is just so great and greatly to be praised."

"He is," Paul agreed.

"Hallelujah," Wendy affirmed. "Did she tell you they're coming up for Thanksgiving?"

"How wonderful!"

"I'd like Paul to come with me to the airport to pick them up tomorrow afternoon, if you can lend him to me for a few hours."

"Of course. I'm just so happy to see you two together again. What a wonderful Thanksgiving! First, President Obama, then your parents' pregnancy, and now the reunion we've all been praying for. We have so much to thank God for."

Paul's mother hugged Wendy, then they both looked at him.

"Thanks for believing in us, Ma, and for being so wise, even when I didn't want to hear what you had to say."

"I thought you always wanted to hear what your mother has to say," Madge quipped.

"I needed to, but want to, that's another story."

"Come here you two." She embraced them both at the same time. Then she held their hands and started to pray. "Our Father, I just want to say thank you. Thank you for bringing our children home for the holidays. Thank you for this new beginning. Help us all to continue to seek you first Lord. Lead them in the path of righteousness. Show them the plans you have for them and help them to walk boldly into the future with you. We pray that you will cover Marcia and her husband as they travel from Jamaica tomorrow. We look forward to spending time together, and let us always remember to praise you, Lord, in all that we are, in all that we say, in all that we do. In Jesus' precious and holy name. Amen."

The airport was crowded, as were the streets lined with traffic with travelers trying to get their destination before the weather changed. The sky was sunny and blue, and at that moment, it was hard to believe the radio announcer who was predicting that by morning, a snowstorm would shut down the airports and make the roadway treacherous for people traveling by car. They felt thankful that the flight arrived on time, ahead of the snow forecasted for that night.

"I certainly don't miss this weather," Devon said, draping one arm over his wife's shoulder. Both of Wendy's parents were sitting in the back seat of the car. Their complexion glowed, darkened by the Jamaican sun-hot.

Wendy noted that her mother was many shades darker than when she lived in New York and often spent cold winter days catching public transportation. "How about you, Mommy? Are you excited to see snow in the short time that you'll be here?"

"Oh sure," Marcia replied, but her voice lacked genuine enthusiasm. She yawned. The pregnancy made her more tired than usual, but she was enjoying being pampered by Devon this time around. It was a stark contrast to her prior experience as a pregnant teenager when she had been so stressed out and alone that she thought she wouldn't survive.

"Tired?" Devon asked, kissing her forehead.

At the same time, Paul asked, "How are you feeling, Mrs. Douglas?"

"Great! Really!" She started giggling as she couldn't suppress another yawn. "I'm just so happy to see you and Wendy together again. We missed you, Paul."

"Thank you," Paul replied feeling deeply touched.

"I could really use a nap," Marcia said, explaining her frequent yawns. "It's funny because I've never been a person to sleep during the day."

"Didn't you sleep on the plane?" Wendy asked her mother.

"No. I was too excited," Marcia replied, "and there was so much distraction." She yawned again and rested her head on her husband's shoulder.

They traveled for a few moments just quietly listening to the radio when a familiar song came on.

Devon sung along for a moment and then said, "I hear this fellow wants to marry my daughter. Paul, what do you think of that?"

Paul chuckled, but kept his eye on the road. Traffic was bumper to bumper, stopping frequently, and he tried to be careful not to run into the car in front of him. "Yes, he does, Mr. Douglas. The question is how do you feel about that, Sir?"

"Ooh." Wendy looked over her shoulder at her father. The car might not be the ideal place for a heart to heart discussion, but it was where she, Paul, and her father had had most of theirs. She still remembered that when she was in high school her father had interrogated them about their love life because he had a hard time believing that they were really saving themselves for marriage.

Devon smiled and took a moment to think before he answered. He was glad Marcia had dozed off because she would probably interject. "I haven't decided yet, Paul. I love you like a son. Like I told you when you called us in Jamaica the other day, you never need to be out of touch with us. My wife and I are always here for you. When it comes to marrying my daughter though, you need to show me some stability. First, you could barely wait to finish high school before you wanted to marry her, then you ran off and got engaged to someone else, and now—fresh off that engagement—you want to marry Wendy again. That's too fickle for me."

Wendy couldn't speak up for Paul at that moment. He needed to handle her father's comments himself, and she was curious to hear what he had to say.

"I made a mistake," Paul said. His eyes met Devon's in the rearview mirror. "Once we get back to the house, I'll be happy to sit down with you face to face, Mr. Douglas. I love Wendy. I always have. I always will. I was foolish to get into a relationship with anyone else, and I'm sorry."

Wendy looked over at him sympathetically.

Devon wasn't so easily impressed. "Just how involved did you get, Son? You had to be deeply involved with this other woman to ask her to marry you. How intimate was that relationship?"

Again, Paul's eyes found Devon's in the rearview mirror. They might as well have been sitting face to face because Paul could feel Devon's intense scrutiny.

"Constance and I spent a lot of time together. From the start, we bonded over music, and she ended up being my agent. She's Bill Channing's daughter and well connected."

"So you used her to build your music career, a career that you expressed no interest in a few years ago."

"Dad!"

"It's okay, Wendy. I didn't use Constance, Mr. Douglas. Our relationship benefited her tremendously. She showed that she has a knack for finding new talent and marketing it to the max. She took me, a nobody in the music industry, and made me into a star—granted I'll probably be remembered as a one-hit wonder. Anyway, she made a name for herself in doing that. She has me on tour locally, doing gigs until the end of the school year, and I'm going to finish what I started because dropping out now would hurt her reputation. I've asked her not to add any shows that have not already been scheduled."

"So you and your ex-fiancée will still be spending a lot of time together. What's to stop you from trying to maintain two relationships?"

Wendy's eyes popped. She felt incredulous, yet thankful, that her father dared to ask those questions.

"For starters, Constance doesn't want to have anything to do with me personally, Mr. Douglas. She is not into sharing her man, and I have never been able to hide my love for Wendy. When we were together, Constance considered Wendy to be a threat to our relationship." He used every chance driving would allow him to make eye contact with Wendy's father in the rearview mirror. "I was unforgiving and stubborn and selfish. And the consequence is that Wendy and I were apart for two years. Wendy has forgiven me, and I believe God has forgiven me." He paused. "Don't forget, Sir, I'm still trying to get into heaven, and I can proudly say I still haven't fornicated. Praise the Lord!"

Devon maintained a serious expression, but he wanted to laugh. It was so uncommon to hear a young man proudly profess his virginity. Strangely enough, he didn't think Paul was lying.

"That's a conviction God laid on my heart a long time ago, and although I love Wendy, I abstained even when I was upset with her because that's something I promised God." Paul sighed. "I can't wait to marry Wendy and fulfill the promises we made to God and to each other." He looked over at Wendy as he mentioned marriage.

Wendy smiled back at him. She liked the way he was handling her father's interrogation.

"Whoa, young stallion," Devon said, tapping him on the shoulder. "You seem sincere enough, but you still need a cooling off period between your last engagement and the next one."

Paul didn't argue. He knew that his actions would be more convincing than words in securing Mr. Douglas's permission to marry his daughter.

A noisy welcome party smothered them with hugs and kisses as they entered the house in the Bronx.

The twins ran circles in and out and around the grownups as they greeted each other.

"Back again," Steve said as he shook Devon's hand and gave him a quick man-hug.

"Yes, Father," Devon replied, using the paternal reference affectionately to refer to his cousin-in-law, as he had since Steve became the father of twins born to his wife Blossom.

"Girl, you are glowing!" Blossom squealed and embraced her cousin Marcia. "I need some shades to look at you, girl. Between the Jamaican sun-hot and the pregnancy, you are just radiating sunshine. You look good."

"Well, thank you. Praise God. You're looking good yourself. Love the hair cut. It fits you." Marcia grinned as Blossom twirled around to model her new look.

"Come here let me look at you, child," Aunt Pat demanded impatiently. She wrapped her arms around her niece and gave her a tight squeeze. "Let me see you good," she said as she stepped back releasing Marcia and scrutinizing her from head to toe. "Boy, it looks like Jamaica really agree with you. You never look so good when you left here."

"What do you expect, Dear?" Uncle Trevor asked his wife. "She is in love, and it looks like her husband is really taking good care of her." He turned his attention to Devon and hugged him.

Aunt Pat grunted. "He better take good care of her, yes." She squinted her eyes at Devon in a loving threat.

Just then, Paul and Wendy brought in the last of Devon and Marcia's luggage.

"Thanks, Paul," Devon said, giving him a quick man-hug. He realized now that he had been treating Paul the way Aunt Pat had always treated him. She seemed to expect the worse from him, basing her expectations on his past transgressions and not on the many things he had done since then to show how much he loved Marcia and Wendy. He recognized a parallel in Paul's life, and realized that Paul deserved the chance to prove that his declarations of love for Wendy were sincere. Devon decided that he would go easier on Paul from then on.

CHAPTER NINETEEN

Sergio spent the night before Thanksgiving baking pies. He spurned frozen pies and readymade ingredients for fresh produce and homemade crusts. He immersed himself in the tasks of peeling sweet potatoes and boiling apples, kneading dough and shaping each crust. As he worked, he cleaned. Once the pies were in the oven, he seasoned up the meat. He planned to wake early to bake the turkey and macaroni and cheese, to fry fish and chicken, to cook up collard greens and rice, to toss a salad, and to juice fruits and carrots for a punch.

Repeat guests knew they didn't need to bring anything but their appetite, but many brought an item out of courtesy. The first couple arrived with sparkling cider. Another brought ice cream. By dinner time, the guests had added broccoli and carrot dip, peach cobbler, and wine to the menu.

Sergio served dinner at four o' clock and was about to say grace when the doorbell rang once more. Standing in the doorway was Constance Channing, wearing a white fur hat and jacket and red leather pants.

"Hi," she said shyly. "I was supposed to go to my friend's house in upstate New York, but I couldn't get there before the snowstorm. I hear they're already buried in a foot of snow. May I have dinner here?"

"Come on in. No explanations needed," Sergio said, leading the way. "Everyone, this is Constance."

The open floor plan of his apartment worked well because the crowd spilled over from the kitchen into the living and dining rooms, but with only a half-wall separating them, they could all see each other.

They all joined hands and bowed their heads, as one of Sergio's guests said grace. "Father God, thank you. Thank you for health and strength. Thank you for everyone who is gathered here. We come from different homes and bear different last names, but we are all a part of your family, Father God. Please bless this home that Sergio opens up to us each year.

Continue to fill it with love and good food. Return on to him a blessing for the way he has blessed us on this day. Restore to him all the energy and love he has put into preparing this meal. And may we all be ready when you send back your Son, in Jesus' name. Amen."

"Amen," folks repeated around the room.

The woman who said the prayer hugged Sergio. Matilda James lived in the building and might have been the college's oldest student. She returned to college after her husband passed away. They hadn't been able to have any children, she'd told Sergio, and she suffered from loneliness and depression at home without her husband. Returning to college to complete a degree had given her a new sense of purpose, and keeping pace with her young friends filled her with vitality. She kept watch over Sergio from a distance and was always praying that he would give his heart to the Lord and give up all that womanizing. With his cooking and housekeeping skills, he would make a good husband and father to some nice young lady, if he would only settle down.

"Thank you," Sergio said, as he hugged her.

"No, no. Thank you. As usual, you outdid yourself," she said, waving a hand toward the spread of food, which Sergio had set up buffet style.

"Dig in, folks. Don't be shy," Sergio suggested and returned to the kitchen to get a bucket of ice. While he was in the kitchen, the phone rang.

"Happy Thanksgiving," Sergio said in greeting.

"Happy Thanksgiving to you, my friend."

"What's up, Wendy?"

Wendy had spent the morning helping her family prepare their Thanksgiving feast. As she looked forward to Paul and his mother coming over, her mind drifted to Sergio and the number of times she had cried on his shoulders because she was missing Paul. She rejoiced that she no longer had reason to cry on Sergio's shoulder, but she felt that she couldn't thank him enough for being there when she so desperately needed a friend.

"We're just getting ready to have dinner, so I wanted to give you a quick call to say thanks for being such a faithful friend."

Sergio halted for a moment, deeply moved. Then he joked, "You're probably the only woman I know who would call me faithful."

Wendy giggled. "Maybe, right now, but I have a feeling that's going to change one day soon."

"They say, once a player, always a player."

"No, my brother. You always have a choice. I've been praying for you for a good while now, and I know prayer changes things."

"Okay, Holy Roller."

"No need to thank me. Save me some pie or something. Okay?"

"We'll see."

Wendy hung up the phone with Sergio and went to shower and

change for dinner. All of their lives together, she never worried about her appearance when she was with Paul. With them, it had always been friendship first, but on that night, she felt like she wanted to impress him.

She wore a yellow dress that warmed her dark complexion. The dress had a high collar in the back and plunged to a sweetheart neckline in front. It clung to her waist and accentuated her hips. She swept her hair up in the back and allowed a few tresses to fall loosely against her face. Colorful makeup didn't suit her personality, so she opted for a sheer lip gloss and translucent mascara.

She was almost ready when she heard the doorbell ring and her Uncle Steve ran downstairs to answer it. She heard Paul and his mother's voices and the sound of footsteps ascending the stairs. Moments later, she heard a light knock at the door.

"I'm coming," she called out. She slipped on a pair of heels over her stocking-clad feet and opened the door.

"Wow!" Paul exclaimed, as he felt his heart do a somersault. Wendy had always looked beautiful to him, but tonight, she looked stunning. He crossed his right arm across his heart and crooned, "There could never be more beautiful you," a line from Johnny Diaz's hit song.

She smiled back at him, and felt tears sting the back of her eyes. She looked over the crewneck shirt, sports jacket and slacks Paul wore, and said, "You look handsome yourself, Mr. Superstar."

Paul shook his head. He grasped each of Wendy's hands. "The last thing I want to be with you is a superstar. If I could rewind the last two years, that's one of the things I would change..."

Wendy hugged him and he held her close.

"If I hadn't made so many mistakes, then your father would take me seriously when I say I want to marry you."

"I know. We both made mistakes." She leaned back and looked into his eyes. "Our future together begins right now."

They kissed.

Paul took her hand, but before he led her up the stairs, he said, "No more detours."

She agreed. "No more detours."

Conversation at the dinner table centered on what life in Jamaica was like for Marcia and Devon. Everyone had questions about how the couple had adjusted to living on the tropical island after living in New York for so many years. Devon had visited Jamaica frequently during those years, often spending time working with his parents at their hotel. Marcia, on the other hand, had experienced a hiatus of almost two decades. She left Jamaica when Wendy was a baby and didn't return until after Wendy's high school graduation.

"You guys are what I miss most about being in New York," she said. "I mean, when we have a family gathering here, look at the crowd. When we get together in Jamaica, it's just me, Devon, and his mom."

"You've got to miss New York though," said Steve. "In many ways, it's still the capital of the world, with its Broadway theaters, fashion district, Wall Street..."

"True, but those things weren't a central part of my life. Working and going to college, riding the subway late at night, and hurrying to get home in the freezing cold. That was my norm, and I certainly don't miss that. I'm so pampered now in comparison. I can't thank Devon enough. Praise the Lord!"

"What's it like having your own maid?" Paul asked.

"Not a maid; a domestic helper. Someone who helps out around the house," Marcia explained.

"That's a gross misrepresentation of your lifestyle, Missy," Blossom interjected. "They have a chauffeur, who they call a driver. They have a gardener. They have a housekeeper who supervises the domestic helpers. Shall I go on?"

"It came with the territory," Devon said, offering further explanation. "After my father died, I stepped into his shoes, inheriting the hotel and all the perks and responsibilities that go with it. Marcia is playing a similar role to my mother's in the early years of my parents' marriage. So if it sounds extravagant, we didn't create that lifestyle, but I'm glad Marcia is enjoying it."

"Who wouldn't?" Blossom and Paul's mother asked in unison.

"I take none of it for granted," Marcia said. "Praise the Lord! Hallelujah! Thank you, Jesus!"

"So how is business since you opened the villas?" Uncle Trevor asked.

"It's been pretty good," Devon said. "Thank God. It'll be a long time before we make back the money we invested, but as you know, it's Dad's legacy; the fulfillment of his dream."

"What a shame that he never lived to see it," Aunt Pat stated. "You would make him proud."

"Thank you, Aunt Pat," Devon said, unable to mask his surprise. He grinned broadly. "That's the nicest thing you've ever said to me."

Aunt Pat grunted and savored a piece of turkey smothered in gravy.

"It's the truth," Uncle Trevor said, adding to his wife's compliment. "We're really proud of you, Devon. You're handling your business well, and you're taking good care of your family. God never makes a mistake."

"Thanks. And to quote my wife: Praise the Lord! Hallelujah! Thank you, Jesus!"

Uncle Trevor looked over at Paul. "Young man, all that talk you've been talking about marriage, you have a lot to learn. If you want an example of the type of husband we want for Wendy, you need to look no further than my two sons-in-law."

Paul responded quickly with another compliment. "I'd add you to the top of that list, Uncle Trevor. I've grown up watching you take care of this family, and I think you set the best example of all."

"I second that," Devon said.

"So say all of us," Steve agreed.

Wendy realized Paul had racked up some brownie points with that compliment, but she knew he spoke sincerely. After sharing over fifty years of marriage fulfillment with his wife, Uncle Trevor reigned as king in Ever After, where Steve and Devon were young princes.

Uncle Trevor nodded modestly, and deflected the attention back to Devon. "So tell me more about the business, Devon. I hear you all had the Prime Minister at your hotel on election night."

"Yes, he was among the dignitaries who assembled in our hotel to watch Senator Barack Obama trump his opponents," Devon said. "The island was so involved in the election, you'd think it was happening locally."

"It was like that across the globe," offered Steve.

"Do you want to hear the best part," Marcia added.

Everyone looked at her.

"We're planning an inauguration ball!"

"Get out!" Blossom exclaimed.

"Let me get this straight," interjected Steve, expressing as much surprise as his wife. "The United States has an election. We call Jamaica from our house in New York where we're watching the election on TV, and you're overseas on an island that is not a US territory having an election night party."

Devon and Marcia nodded.

"And now you're planning a ball to celebrate the US president's inauguration," Blossom added. "You are just living a fabulous life."

"It sounds glamorous, but it's a lot of hard work," Marcia explained.

"And we can't take any credit for these ideas," Devon informed them. "Do you remember my friend Troy and his wife Tricia?"

"Of course," Uncle Trevor replied, and others nodded.

"Well, Troy is still my attorney and a business partner. Combine that with Tricia's knack for publicity. When they're not too busy making babies, they're very good at making money."

"How many children do they have now?" Blossom asked. The twins had napped through the first part of dinner and were now awake and hungry. She and Steve cut their food into tiny pieces and fed them, but everyone else was willing to help.

"Tricia just had her third child," Marcia responded. "She loves being a mother and spends a lot time of time with her children, but she is still elitist and extravagant. She knows how to plan a party that will attract all the local VIPs and generate a tremendous amount of media coverage. I'm out of my element in that area, but for her, it's a gift."

"Tricia and Troy are great partners, as are Marcia and I," Devon said, holding his wife's hand. "Hospitality is our specialty. We let Troy and Tricia handle the fanfare, while we roll out the red carpet."

"The inauguration balls here will be televised," said Steve. "Perhaps you could have yours recorded, so we could watch it one day. I'm curious to see what that's like."

"Perhaps we could go down for it, honey," Blossom suggested.

"And do what with our kids?"

"Bring them," Marcia said. "Our villas have great nannies on staff. We could assign one to take care of the twins, so you guys could enjoy the ball."

Blossom loved the sound of that.

Steve was more skeptical about a stranger watching his children, even if it was a hired nanny. "We'll get back to you on that," he told Devon.

CHAPTER TWENTY

Sergio woke up on the Sunday morning following Thanksgiving with an unfamiliar desire to go to church. Wendy hadn't prompted him to attend. She had invited him many times before and he had declined. The college campus was still pretty deserted. Sergio expected that most of the students would return that afternoon into the evening.

He pinned up his locks in a ponytail and donned a suit. This was a chance for him to fulfill his independent study requirement. The role of the African American church was a course of required study in his major. Most students fulfilled the requirement well before senior year. Sergio had procrastinated, determined to avoid a course that would require him to spend time in church. Finally, he convinced the department chairperson to allow him to take the course as an independent study. His grade would be based on a single twenty-page paper about the church's role in the community. Sergio had researched the topic by reading extensively and conducting interviews, and finally on that morning, he was going to set foot inside of a church.

Sergio stood outside the dark stone building and stared up at the steeple. He noted that right on the very top was a cross. Inside, he listened to the preacher talk about how Jesus died on a cross, so that our sins may be forgiven. "Therefore, if any man is in Christ, he is a new creature: old things are passed away; behold, all things are become new." He followed along in the Bible Wendy had given him as the preacher read from second Corinthians, chapter five, verse seventeen.

The preacher talked about how a person can find peace by nailing all their cares to the cross and leaving them there. As the preacher stated each infraction, he drove a nail into a large wooden cross, fastening a sheet of paper bearing the words there: "Sex abuse. Substance abuse. Unforgiveness. Bitterness. Fornication. Adultery..." Each loud thud pierced deeper and deeper into Sergio's heart. All his life he had locked away the anger and bitterness he felt toward his parents for bringing him into the world to suffer and fend for himself, for introducing him and his siblings to a life of crime, and then abandoning them in foster care when they got caught doing what they had been taught. From an early age, he had enjoyed intimacy, but shunned commitment, afraid to love any one woman because his own mother had never loved him. Her substance abuse had robbed her of the capacity to love.

Sergio had built for himself a fort that allowed him to share his body, but shield his heart. It offered shallow pleasure but lacked deep fulfillment. He had always longed for the type of family he watched on the Cosby show during his youth. The images of the Obama family had renewed that longing with greater fervency. He could no longer keep the pain of his past locked up behind that fort that guarded his heart. He needed to nail it to that cross and leave it there.

The preacher invited the congregation to write down the things that caused them pain on a piece of paper and fold the paper if they wanted to keep it between them and God. Then he invited them to come forward and nail their burdens to the cross.

Sergio felt like he was outside of himself as he stood up and walked forward. He felt tears streaming down his face. Tears seeped from his eyes, but they felt like they weren't his.

"Nail it and leave it there, Son," he heard the preacher say as he pounded a nail into the cross. "Jesus died for you too. Jesus loves you and will carry you through."

The choir started singing the hymn, "What a friend we have in Jesus. All our sins and grief to bear. What a privilege to carry everything to God in prayer."

Many of the congregants who had nailed their burdens to the cross knelt down at the altar. Sergio found himself there among them, although he didn't feel like his legs had carried him there. The preacher prayed for them and anointed their foreheads with oil.

As they were returning to their seats, a woman begged the preacher for a chance to testify. The preacher handed her the microphone and she spoke candidly about how God had delivered her from a life destroyed by drug abuse. "He didn't leave me to die," she said sobbing tearfully. Her voice conveyed both joy and pain as she explained how she spent time in detox, and a halfway house, and a sanctuary for battered women before finally getting her own apartment. She had tried and failed many times before, but this time was different. The court agreed and had given her back her baby girl who had just celebrated her second birthday.

"By the grace of God, I'm going to be a good mother to her," she promised. "Lord knows I wish I could make it up to every other child who had a mother like me."

Sergio saw his mother in the woman who testified. He prayed that God had delivered her from substance abuse by now and that she hadn't suffered and died in that lifestyle. His mind drifted to Dré 's mother and he prayed that she too would be delivered from that lifestyle. And he asked God to help him change his lifestyle. Promiscuity could literally be hidden under the covers where no one would see its destructiveness. Diseases and broken families had been documented in impersonal statistics, but for the first time Sergio admitted that his own promiscuity was destroying his life.

The preacher was inviting anyone who desired membership in the church to meet with one of the elders when Sergio walked out. He wasn't ready to join a church, and didn't know whether he would ever come back to that one. Someone handed him a tract as he was leaving the sanctuary. Big bold letters on the front read, "JESUS SAVES."

Inside his apartment, Sergio read the tract from beginning to end. It ended with a prayer he could pray to invite Jesus to live in his heart. It made reference to Bible verses in Romans and suggested that new believers should read the gospel of John. Sergio opened the Bible and started reading John, beginning at the first chapter. The words leapt off the page. Sergio felt like God was talking directly to him. He fell on his knees in silence. After a while, he stood up and went and took a shower and changed.

That evening, Sergio's cell phone kept lighting up. His women-friends were texting or calling to let him know they were back on campus. He didn't have to be alone tonight and he knew it. The offers seemed tempting. Sergio put on the CD that Paul had recorded. He had never played it before, but like most of the other college students, he owned a signed copy. That Jesus music, as so many of his acquaintances called it, strengthened his resolve not to invite someone over that night.

As the Christmas break approached, students busied themselves studying for final exams. They had research papers to complete and they crammed into the library. Yet it seemed like the more they studied, the more they partied.

"You've got to let the stress out somehow," Kim told Wendy, urging her to party with them for a little while.

She didn't know that Wendy had already planned to meet Paul there because he would be performing one of his songs early in the night.

"Let's go," Wendy said.

Despite Kim's pleading, Wendy's affirmative responsive took her by surprise. "Well, alright then. Let's go. Party over there."

They picked up Donna and headed out of the dorm to the student center. They joined a line and paid the entrance fee. Inside, the music was blasting. They stood on the edge of the crowded dance floor.

"Everybody's here," Kim squealed. She started swaying to the music and a guy came over and asked her to dance.

Soon she and Donna were on the dance floor.

Wendy walked around looking for Paul in the dim light. She saw Sergio who raised his eyebrows in surprise to see her there. Then, they both saw Paul, and Sergio nodded indicating that he understood.

Paul and Constance stood face to face, as Wendy approached. Constance still acted as Paul's agent, so Wendy wasn't surprised to see them like that. She stopped as she got close to them, and didn't try to interrupt their conversation. Constance spotted her first and the change in her facial expression prompted Paul to turn to see who she was looking at. He smiled at Wendy and politely ended his conversation with Constance. Constance felt momentarily slighted, but she bounced back fast by grabbing the most handsome guy she could spot nearby and dragging him onto the dance floor.

"It looks like I might not be performing tonight," Paul stated, his lips close to Wendy's ear.

The music was loud, but she heard him. "Why? What happened?" she asked.

"There was supposed to be a stage show, but the crowd had other ideas. Everybody wants to dance." He extended his arm slightly toward the stage where the more flamboyant dancers were showcasing their skills.

"So, can we leave?"

"Not yet. Constance asked me to stick around, just in case they decide to put on the show on later. We'll get paid, as long as I'm here, but if they call my name and I'm not around, they'll say I reneged on the agreement."

Wendy nodded. Her fifth semester was ending, but this was her first college party. She felt relieved that she hadn't come to one before, as she observed the raunchy dancing. Minus their clothes, some of the couples would be making love on the dance floor. She decided that she wouldn't blend into that behavior.

She and Paul hung out and talked as the minutes turned into hours. It had always been like that between them, so on that night, they enjoyed each other's pure friendship, in spite of the seductive atmosphere around them.

There was a commotion by the door just as the party entered its final hour. It wasn't loud enough to disrupt the dancers, but Wendy and Paul saw Kane storm in and head straight for Sergio and Monique who were dancing with each other. Their bodies were touching as Monique moved her hips suggestively against Sergio's. He leaned forward and said something that made her laugh, his lips next to her ear.

Kane walked right up to them and yanked Monique by her hair. "I'm sick and tired of you disrespecting me like this, woman," he said.

Monique screamed.

"Let her go," Sergio shouted, and punched Kane in the face.

Kane stepped back, shaking his head as he touched his face, examined his fingers and saw blood. He cursed, pulled a gun from his pocket and fired three shots.

Pandemonium broke lose as everyone screamed and scrambled to take cover. Paul sheltered Wendy with his body and forced her to hide behind the refreshment stand. Those who could ran out of the building. Everyone was calling 911 on their cell phones. The presence of campus security did little to calm their fears. The sounds of sirens filled up the night as police surrounded the building. People were crying. Others just stood, looking dazed, in total shock.

Paramedics rushed in, accompanied by police. Police tried to evacuate the building and control the crowd long enough to interview witnesses.

"The suspect is down," Wendy heard them say. "Three victims… gunshot wounds… possible fatalities…"

The words pounded through Wendy's brain as an officer directed her, Paul, and the students who had been hiding with them to exit the building.

Media arrived on the scene, and campus administrators fielded their questions and worked with police to keep them from pestering the students.

Paul wrapped his arms around Wendy as they waited to hear what had happened to Kane, Sergio, and Monique. Wails of grieving and hysterical students rocked the night.

"What song were you going to sing tonight?" Wendy asked Paul.

"Huh?" Paul heard her question but wanted to make sure of what she was really asking.

"What song were you going to sing tonight?"

He named two from his CD.

"Sing them for me."

"Now?" Paul asked, puzzled by her unexpected request.

"Please."

Paul softly began to hum and then to sing songs of praise to God.

Wendy found comfort in the soothing sound of his voice. She listened to the lyrics of the songs which described how Jesus came to save sinners and rescue lost souls. Like everyone else, she and Paul had panicked, and because of the speed with which things happened, no one intervened to try to stop the shooting. Now, it seemed there was nothing they could do. But as she listened to Paul's song she realized that they needed to pray.

Paul sang softly, but the soothing sound of his voice penetrated the night and had a magnetic pull on the people who heard him, and they moved closer. It created a sanctuary amidst the sirens, and the wailing, and the shouts. His words tapered off and he started to hum again.

"We need you, Lord," Wendy began praying. "Father God, in the name of Jesus, we ask that you pour out your Holy Spirit in the midst of this place right now. Please take control of this situation right now, Lord. You said that at the name of Jesus every knee shall bow and every tongue confess that Jesus Christ is Lord. So Father, we intercede right now on behalf of those who know you as their Savior, and on behalf of those who don't know you or have rejected you. Forgive us, Lord. Forgive us, Lord, of this sin called murder. Cleanse us of anger and hatred and strife, Lord Jesus," she cried out louder now, forgetting those around her and appealing to God from her heart with Sergio's face on her mind. "Pour out your life saving power. Save our souls. Fill us with new life…"

Inside the building, the paramedics had pronounced two students dead, but as they placed the second body on a stretcher, one of the paramedics shouted, "Wait a minute. I detect a pulse." He and his partner rushed the stretcher over to the ambulance and covered the patient's face with an oxygen mask.

CHAPTER TWENTY-ONE

Later that morning, Wendy and Paul continued their prayer vigil in the hospital waiting room. Their prayers wouldn't change the fact that Kane had died, but they prayed that he'd had time to repent and that God would save his soul. Monique had been admitted to the hospital where she was being treated for superficial gunshot wounds and was in stable condition, they had learned from the Internet news reports. And Sergio had been shot in the head. The paramedics pronounced him dead on the scene at first, but as they were situating his body on the stretcher, ready to cover his face with a sheet, the paramedic adjusting his arm detected a pulse.

"Hallelujah!" Wendy shouted when she heard. She didn't need a medical explanation. She placed all her faith in God, thanking him for saving her friend's life.

Many students left the college after the incident, but they returned to take their final exams. Grief, depression, and disappointment filled the atmosphere. People counted down the days to the Christmas break and couldn't wait to get away.

Monique vacillated between wanting to use her injuries as an excuse to go home early and wanting to stay around to redeem herself. She blamed herself for what had happened, and Kane's mother had publicly cursed her out, calling her a "scheming and conniving gold-digger." That quote had made it onto the Internet causing Monique to feel like she had been shamed before the world.

Monique arrived at Professor Abbey's last class for the semester, hoping to find sympathy in the faces of her classmates.

"In an attempt to restore normalcy, some professors have forbidden their classes to discuss the incidents of the last few days," Professor Abbey informed the class. "They have tried to proceed with business as usual, completing their syllabus and administering final exams. But as students of history and its impact on people of African descent, students who hunger for knowledge about where we originated, how we got to this point, and where do we go from here, I urge you to find the lesson in the tragedy that happened on our college campus." As he stood before the group, his eyes focused and rested on one student's face before moving to another.

"The media has dubbed the incident a crime of passion, but I challenge you to look at it from another perspective and develop a solution. Violence among teenagers and young adults in urban communities is causing too many black mothers to have to bury their sons. Far too often, it happens to young men who possess a potential for greatness, but succumb to a life of crime. Sometimes, it sneaks into the schoolyard, and on to the college campus, claiming the life of a student who has studied hard and played it straight. Thank God, Monique is still here."

Professor Abbey placed a hand on Monique's head and smiled at her. Then, he stepped away and continued, "But we've lost Kane, and we almost lost Sergio. As students of history, in this election year, you paused to evaluate how far we as a black people have come. You understood the significance of the moment in which this nation elected its first black president. You interviewed grandparents and elders who lived through Jim Crow, segregation, and the terror of the Klu Klux Klan. But I challenge you today to look at the enemy within: this surge in black on black crime among the younger generation in some communities. Somewhere along the way, the younger generation failed to see the value in another black man's life. The same generation that is reaping the greatest benefit from the sacrifices of our ancestors is the same one that is in danger of missing the point, of squandering its opportunities for education and social advancement, and of taking each other's life. How do you—future leaders—propose to solve this problem?"

The students contemplated all that Professor Abbey had said in silence. Professor Abbey gave them time.

Finally, a male student raised his hand.

"Yes, Michael," Professor Abbey acknowledged him.

"What you said is true, Professor Abbey. When you look at the death toll in some communities among young, black men and teenage boys, it's alarming. We've heard Mayor Corey Booker sound the alarm for his community many times. But outside of those communities, nobody cares. I mean, the mothers who are burying their sons care, and the family, and the friends of those victims. But no one assesses it as a comprehensive problem that the country needs to solve."

"Is it?" Professor Abbey asked. "Is the problem one that needs be addressed on the national agenda?"

"Yes," another student replied.

"Cynthia?" Professor Abbey acknowledged her.

She continued, "I think it's everybody's business that so many black and Hispanic mothers have had to bury their sons and daughters due to youth violence. We no longer have to worry about the Klu Klux Klan lynching our sons and daughters and cutting off their lives and their potential. We're doing it to ourselves."

"So how do you stop that? How do you put an end to that epidemic?" Professor Abbey asked.

"I think the communities where this is happening need to deal with it locally," another student suggested. "More police on the streets, better discipline in the schools, and more supervision of adolescents when they are out of school. The people who live with the problem know it best, so they need to fix it. The federal government can't come from outside and fix it for them."

"Valid perspective," Professor Abbey conceded. "However, I want you to put it under the microscope considering all that you have studied during the years you've attended this university. That approach would not have justified people from the North sacrificing their lives to help people in the South overcome the oppression of racial hatred and segregation. Black and white children learned side by side in classrooms in New Jersey, at a time when racial mixing was violently opposed in the South. Instead of ignoring their neighbor's plight and saying it's their problem; let them deal with it, the entire country got involved."

Michael raised his hand again and Professor Abbey nodded. "So, Professor, you're asking us to make a connection between the struggles in the South that claimed the lives of so many young people and the youth violence today. I'm not sure there is a connection."

Professor Abbey explained, "The impact is the same: the tragic destruction of young lives." Professor Abbey paused and allowed his statement to sink in. After a while, he said, "Michael, your grandfather could not even conceive of the idea that a black man would one day become president of the United States. As you described in your paper, he had experienced so much racial hatred while growing up in the South that he was convinced that whites would never allow a black man to become president. In addition, you concluded that your grandfather questioned his own worth and developed an inferiority complex that caused him to give up on his own aspirations. I argue that the same thing is happening to some of our young people today—except that the culprit is not white on black crime. It is black on black crime that is robbing our communities of young people with great potential and desensitizing them to the value of each other's lives. What are you future leaders going to do to solve this problem?"

Some of the students looked at each other.

"I had this assignment prepared long before the tragic shooting that took place on our college campus. If the problem of youth violence is to be addressed locally, then we are part of the local configuration because our college campus is in such close proximity to an urban center where the death toll among young black males is high. Many of you are success stories, having been born in the heart of a violent community, but you managed to elevate yourselves through education and athletic achievements. The tragic link for Kane and Sergio is that they escaped the violence of the streets but…" Professor Abbey extended his hand. His body language said, "You know the rest of the story."

"Some are calling the movement to engage all of our youth, to rescue them from the perils of gang activity and violent crime the new civil rights movement. Yes, blacks have achieved much in America, the pinnacle of which is our newly elected President Barack Obama—but some of our children have been left behind. As long as our youth continue to disproportionately fill up the jail cells, and youth violence continues to rise among black youth while it is declining among the general population, we all have a problem. It is incumbent upon you, future leaders, to develop a solution."

Professor Abbey walked around the room and distributed a packet to each student. "Your grade for the next level of this course will be based on one paper that you will have the chance to write and revise repeatedly during the course of the spring semester. Your reading assignment for the winter break includes *The Covenant with Black America*, by Tavis Smiley, and Bill Cosby's book *Come On People*."

Students perused the papers they received from Professor Abbey.

"History will probably record Bill Cosby's call out meetings in urban areas as part of this new civil rights movement, along with the comprehensive effort made by Mayor Corey Booker and other urban leaders who have tried to tackle the problem of violence in their communities. Reverend Dr. Martin Luther King, like many of the leaders of the Civil Rights Movement of the 1950s and 1960s, rose up out of the black church. Some folks argue that the church has fallen asleep. I challenge you, future leaders, to evaluate whether we as a people can really be satisfied that we have moved ahead, when so many of our youth have been left behind."

After class, Monique found the sympathy she was looking for in her classmates as they stopped to ask how she was doing, and offered to share their notes with her from the few classes she had missed.

Paul and Wendy walked out together.

"Professor Abbey was on a roll today," Wendy said.

"On a serious mission," Paul agreed. "But how can we disagree with him?"

"There is such a dichotomy between those of us who make it and those who don't," Wendy stated.

"Yeah. Like Dré, those who don't make it literally get eaten alive." There was a catch in Paul's voice as he mentioned Dré.

Wendy empathized with Paul even more now, after coming so close to losing Sergio. "Sometimes, when folks make it, they never look back and lend a hand to pull someone else up behind them," she said. "Perhaps, if more people cared and took time to give back it would help."

Paul sighed. "There is no simple solution. It's funny that we got into this program because we were so determined to go to Africa, but I think God is showing us that there is a lot of work to be done right here in the United States."

"You're right about that." Wendy agreed and then she changed the subject. "I'm going to stop by the produce store and head over to visit Sergio. Do you want to come?"

"I can't. I'm meeting Constance now remember. Her father is in the city and he's sending a car to pick her up, so they can have dinner together."

"Oh. How grand!" Wendy said, with mock sophistication. "And have you already met the one and only Bill Channing?"

"No, actually I haven't. He seems to keep a pretty tight schedule and Constance doesn't see him often. She wanted me to go with her today."

"So, go. I'm going to hang out with Sergio for a while. You go hobnob with the media execs who made your career."

"Wendy."

"Seriously." Wendy giggled. "Go. I don't mind."

"I don't think it's appropriate. Call me later. I'll probably be in my room."

"Okay. Say hi to Constance."

"Yeah. Tell Sergio I said what's up."

Wendy arrived at Sergio's building just as his neighbor Matilda James was unlocking the door to go inside.

"Hey, Matty," Wendy called out to her.

Matilda held the door open for her. "Hello there, Wendy. What do you have there?"

"I picked up a few groceries for Sergio. Have you seen him today?"

"No. I've been out all day, but I'll stop by to visit with you now, if you think he won't mind."

"I don't think he would. Come on."

Although Sergio had given her a key to his apartment while he was in the hospital, Wendy knocked at the door and waited for him to answer.

"If it isn't my two favorite ladies," Sergio said, as he opened the door.

He attempted to take the bags from Wendy.

She slipped by him. "I've got this," she said and headed for the kitchen.

Sergio turned to Matilda and kissed her on the cheek.

"How are you doing, Son?" She had taken to calling him that since the incident. She and Wendy had convinced the nurses at the hospital that they were Sergio's family. He had no biological family around. Matilda told them she was his mother and Wendy claimed to be his sister.

"I'm good," Sergio said. He walked ahead of her to the living room and sat down.

"I don't believe you," Matilda said frankly, and stood in front of him with her arms folded. "Young man, you have cooked and cleaned for everyone in this building, at least once a year. Please give us a chance to take care of you."

"I can take care of myself."

"I'm sure you can, but you don't have to." She looked into his eyes.

Sergio dared not look away. He wondered now if this was what it would have been like to have a real mother, a bossy lady trying to get in his business and tell him what to do. He liked Matilda and trusted her.

"You have a headache," Matilda observed. "Wendy, bring me a glass of water."

"Yes, Ma'am," Wendy replied from the kitchen.

"What have you eaten today?" Matilda demanded to know.

"A little somethin' something'. Nothing much."

"I'm going to make you some soup. Vegetable. It may not taste as good as anything you'd make, but it'll be nutritious. Okay?"

Sergio smiled, thinking: Who would have thought that meddling Matilda would become Mother Matilda in his life. "Thank you."

"And I'll toast some bread to go with that," Wendy said, reaching over Matilda's shoulder with the glass of water. Cooking was not one of her strengths, but she could make toast.

Matilda left Wendy and Sergio in the living room and went into the kitchen to start cooking.

"Where is your medication?" Wendy asked.

"In the bathroom in the medicine cabinet."

Wendy retrieved it and held it out to Sergio. "Here, take this."

"I don't want to."

She flopped down in the chair beside him. "Rough day?"

"Yes."

Wendy was quiet for a while. Then she said, "The doctor said your headaches would come and go." She held his hand and in vintage Wendy style, she began to pray. "Father God, thank you for Sergio. Thank you for saving his life, God. We heard what the doctor said, and we just come to you as the chief physician, Lord, asking you to heal these headaches. Please take away the pain. We can't thank you enough for sparing Sergio's life, Lord, and we just ask that you forgive us of our sins. Continue to comfort Kane's family, Lord, and to heal and strengthen Monique. We thank you and praise you in everything, Father God, in Jesus' name. Amen."

"Amen," Matilda confirmed from the kitchen.

"I like how you pray," Sergio said, smiling at her. Prior to the incident, he had taken those prayers for granted. They meant so much more to him now. "Thanks for always praying for me."

Wendy shrugged.

"Really." Sergio's voice was husky. "I see where your prayers have really made a difference in my life."

"Praise God, Sergio. God doesn't always give us what we ask for…"

They were quiet for a little while before Sergio said, "Something happened to me."

Wendy looked at him, curious to hear what one thing he would identify. So much had happened to Sergio in such a short time. The paramedics had pronounced him dead when they arrived at the party. Then, they detected a pulse and rushed him to the hospital for surgery. He made a miraculous recovery, but they had to shave his head causing him to lose the locks that he had worn proudly since his teenage years. He looked different. A baldy conveyed a different personality from his trademark dreadlocks. Most importantly though, it was just good to see him alive.

"Spiritually, something's happening," he told Wendy. "It started on Thanksgiving Sunday when I went to church."

"You did what?"

"I did. It was weird. I went for my independent study course, but I also felt a pull. The service was moving. It's like I reconciled with my father."

"I thought you never knew your father."

"Not that father, dingy," Sergio said, jokingly calling her dumb. "You know, Father God. The one you're always talking to, even when people want you to shut up."

Wendy laughed. "Oh you're funny. So you've been talking to my father."

"No. I've been talking my father. I accepted that he cares about me, in spite of everything."

Wendy felt her heart sing, thankful and amazed at what Sergio was saying.

"It's a lot. I can't really explain it to you. It's like God is forcing me to make a change in my life… changing it for the better, although you couldn't tell by looking at me."

Wendy smiled. "You look pretty good to me. I don't think you ever looked better."

He chuckled. "If only I could feel as good as I look."

"You'll get there. God didn't bring you this far to leave you."

"That's the thing. I have no doubt that God is doing something good for me in the midst of all this." He pointed to the bandage on his head.

"I understand. When you went to church the other day, did you get saved?"

"How does one get saved?"

"If you confess with your mouth the Lord Jesus, and believe in your heart that God raised him from the dead, you will be saved. Romans, chapter ten, verse nine. That's in the Bible."

"I have been reading that Bible you gave me," Sergio said, looking directly at her. "For the first time in my life I feel like God is speaking to me. When I read, it's like the words are jumping off the page with a message just for me."

"Hallelujah! Keep reading then, Sergio."

He nodded.

Matilda came out to the living room and said, "The soup's cooking. I put the timer on. Wendy, you can occasionally stir the pot. I'm going down to my apartment. Perhaps, I'll be back. Call me if you need me."

"Thanks, Matty. You're the best," Sergio said.

"Listen to me, Sergio Rayford. If anything worse happens to you and I'm right here and you don't call me, I'll be so mad at you. Don't you hesitate to call me," Matilda said, wagging her finger at him. "I don't have a child. You don't have a mother, so as far as I'm concerned, God made us for each other. You are my son, and I love you, so don't hesitate to call me."

"Yes, Mother," Sergio said grinning. He could sense Matilda's sincerity, and he needed it. He couldn't remember ever feeling so vulnerable. Physically, he needed their help, but emotionally, he felt like it was their love that would get him through this. Before the incident, he had asked God to help him let go of the hurt feelings he had buried inside, feelings caused by abandonment and betrayal by his mother. Now, it was like God was filling up the void that removing those negative feelings left with love; true love.

"Thanks, Matty," Wendy said, as she walked her out.

"You know, you'd make a good daughter-in-law."

"Daughter. My heart belongs to Paul."

"I tell you that Paul Chambers is a lucky guy." Matilda walked away.

Wendy stopped to stir the soup before returning to the living room.

"So what's happening on campus?"

Wendy told him about Professor Abbey's assignment.

"It's hard to write a prescription to fix people," Sergio said, shaking the bottle with prescription medicine while he spoke. "I'm not saying we mustn't try to find solutions, but I think it takes more than what meets the eye to bring about a revolution."

Wendy looked attentively at him.

"All that prayer stuff that you do," Sergio continued, "I think God has something to do with any change."

"Who's the Holy Roller now?"

"Still you," Sergio said, chuckling. "So how is your boyfriend?"

"He's great. We were in class together. Then, he went to meet Constance."

"How ironic is that? He's out with his ex and here you are alone with me."

"We trust each other," Wendy said and returned to the kitchen to stir the soup again. There were only a few minutes left on the timer, so she stayed there until it was ready. She brought Sergio his soup on a tray.

"Thank you." He closed his eyes for a moment.

Wendy guessed that he was saying grace.

"That Matty sure can burn," Sergio said, as he tasted the soup. "This is good. You should have some."

"I will." Wendy got herself a bowlful and joined him.

CHAPTER TWENTY-TWO

Wendy joined her parents in Jamaica for Christmas. She and Paul had grown up spending every Christmas and Easter together in the church they attended with their mothers. The first time they spent Easter apart was shortly after Wendy met her father for the first time during her senior year of high school. Her decision to go to Jamaica with her father back then had been one of the factors that led her and Paul to break up. This time, there was a mutual understanding between them about the need for them to go their separate ways for the holiday. Paul stayed in the Bronx with his mother, but he called Wendy at a few minutes to midnight on Christmas Eve, so they could welcome Christmas Day together on the phone.

"What's it like spending Christmas at a hotel?" Paul asked.

"We're not at the hotel. We're at my parent's house, even though I was surprised to see how many guests have checked into the hotel for the holidays. The villas are also hosting a couple family reunions. They are mostly people from up north opting for Jamaican sun-hot over the comfort of home."

"Is it really hot there now?" Paul could mentally picture Wendy running around in shorts and t-shirt instead of the heavy coat she had been wearing when he drove her to the airport in New York. They'd had a winter wonderland since the Thanksgiving snow storm, and although it hadn't snowed again, it was cold outside.

"It's pretty warm here," Wendy informed him. "The nights cool off though. You can feel the Christmus breeze," Wendy said, substituting a "u" sound at the end of Christmas in an effort to sound Jamaican.

"I like your accent," Paul said, chuckling. "Cool runnings."

Wendy laughed. "Okay. I see you've been watching your Disney movies."

"You can't blame a guy for trying."

"No, Sir, but you need to come on down here, so you can acquire some authentic Jamaican flavor," Wendy said, now sounding more British than Jamaican or American. The versatility in switching back and forth between the Queen's English and Jamaican patois was also typical of Jamaicans. She longed to share with Paul all that she had grown to know and love about Jamaica in the years since she met her father.

"Once we get married, we'll be spending time together there," Paul suggested. "Perhaps, Christmas in Jamaica will become a part of our family tradition."

Wendy liked the sound of that. "Yes, but we'll have to convince your mother to come with us. We wouldn't want her to be alone for the holidays."

Paul felt satisfied that Wendy loved him and she cared about his mother. A year ago, he had scarcely taken time to spend with his mother during the holidays. He was a rising star with a music career, and Constance had him booked for performances throughout the winter break. He'd felt so heady from the spotlight that he had lost sight of the things that were most important, like being there for his mother, a widow who was otherwise alone for the holidays. Paul liked the fact that Wendy helped him stay grounded.

"What time are you going to see Sergio tomorrow?" Wendy asked. She had made Paul promise her that he would visit Sergio, so he could give her a first-hand report on how he was doing.

"We'll probably head over there in the early afternoon. We don't want to get stuck in the evening traffic. I touched base with him today. He didn't sound too enthusiastic," Paul said.

"Sergio is like that. He does a lot for people, but doesn't like for others to go out of their way for him. Please don't let him talk you out of the visit."

"I won't," Paul promised. He and Sergio still weren't friends, but Wendy had unofficially adopted Sergio as her brother, and Paul would do just about anything for Wendy. In addition, even strangers were concerned about Sergio's health, having become acquainted with him from the news stories about the tragedy. Paul's mother was one of them and she was looking forward to meeting Sergio on Christmas Day. "Don't worry. I'll call you tomorrow night and let you know how your brother is doing."

"Thank you. Have I told you how much I appreciate you?" Wendy asked.

"I know you do. Guess what?"

"What?"

"Merry Christmas!" Paul exclaimed.

Wendy glanced at the clock in her room and saw that it was past midnight. "Merry Christmas! Happy birthday, Jesus!"

The New Year arrived with excitement mounting over the inauguration of the first African American president of the United States. Sergio felt his depressed feelings evaporate to be replaced by a sense of determination to rebuild his health in time to attend the Inauguration ceremony in Washington, DC. He was one of a select group of honor students who had been chosen to represent the university at the event. He tried to make the best of each day, conscious that like Kane, his life might have ended suddenly between Election and Inauguration Day. And taking a cue from Wendy, he prayed that God would put a hedge of protection around the incoming president and his family. Like many students of American history, he felt concern that enough racial hatred still existed to threaten the incoming president's life.

Classes wouldn't resume until after the Inauguration, but some students returned early hoping to get on the bus to Washington, DC. It seemed like everyone wanted a place at the Inauguration, with or without an invitation. Churches and community groups organized bus trips. Individuals and families made plans to be present in the nation's capital on that day.

Government authorities became concerned about crowd control and issued warnings that limited access would be granted to Capitol Hill. After watching the news reports, the college administrators made the decision that their bus would leave on Saturday afternoon.

Wendy and Paul drove over to see Sergio on Saturday morning. They prayed together with Matilda in his apartment before they walked Sergio to the college parking lot to get on the bus.

"Thanks for carrying my bag, man," Sergio said to Paul.

"No problem, man." Paul gave Sergio a pound, fist to fist. "Go make history for the rest of us."

"Right!" Sergio couldn't hide his excitement.

Wendy grinned. She understood how much this opportunity meant to him. She squeezed him tightly as he gave her a hug. "You be careful now, Sergio."

"I'll be fine," Sergio reassured her.

"Don't be too proud to ask for help if you need it," Matilda and Wendy advised him.

Sergio chuckled and looked to Paul for help. Yes, he had wanted family for the security and fulfillment it seemed to provide. Yet, he was also learning that having family meant losing the space and independence he was accustomed to, all because these people cared about him.

"Sergio knows how to take care of himself, ladies. Give him a break," Paul said.

"Call us when you get there."

"Send us pictures from your cell phone."

Sergio climbed the steps onto the bus.
Wendy, Paul, and Matilda waited until the bus drove away.

The atmosphere was pungent with intense emotions, as the bus got on the New Jersey Turnpike and headed south. Sergio sat in his seat with his attention fixed on the television, watching the images of President-elect Barack Obama and Vice President-elect Joe Biden on their train ride from Philadelphia to Washington, DC. He found himself praying for their safety, like he had never prayed for anyone before, as they mingled with the crowds of people who lined up for miles for a chance to glimpse the black man who would be president. Elderly people, babies in their parents' arms, and every age group in between pressed forward in an orderly fashion for a chance to shake the presidential party's hands. And the two men made themselves accessible, touchable, in a way that evoked appreciation in the admiring faces that gazed back at them.

Students around him were chatting, but rather than heading up the group discussions as he would have in the past, Sergio remained quiet and reflective. He wanted to shake the President's hand, and he wanted to record the moment to tell his children about how he almost didn't live to witness that historical moment when the President was sworn in, but God gave him a second chance. Sergio gazed out of the window for a moment at the thought of children; his children. Now, he knew he really needed to reign in his emotions. He had not wanted children before. He had meticulously tried to make sure that none of the women he slept with would become pregnant with his baby. Nowadays, he found himself longing to start a family and give his children everything his own parents never gave him. He almost wished Paul and Wendy hadn't worked things out because she was the only female in his life that he would consider marrying.

The jewelry case with the engagement ring rubbed against Paul's leg as he walked with Wendy back to the car in the college's parking lot. The dormitories where they made their on-campus home stood closed and empty, so after Sergio's bus left, Paul and Wendy walked Matilda to her apartment building, then returned to their car to drive back to New York.

They had been spending all of their free time together since Wendy's return from Jamaica. The bond between them congealed like over two years of separation had never taken place, but they were young adults now, and desired more than just friendship. Up until their teenage years, their closest friendships had been with each other. The past two years had changed that, as Paul dated and became engaged to Constance, and Wendy developed a tight bond with Sergio. Neither of those relationships had involved physical intimacy, and greater tension pulled at Paul and Wendy now to share an experience that neither one had shared with anyone else.

As Paul started the car, he recognized the melody of the song playing on the radio. The song Cover Me, by the young male trio 21:03, with Fred Hammond, Smokie Norful, and J. Moss, was a theme song for his life. The song reminded him to constantly be in a state of prayer, and made him thankful that people like his mother and their pastor, and Wendy, were always praying for him. He let the car run for a while to warm up and turned to face Wendy.

"I never stopped praying for you all the while that we were apart," Paul said.

"And I never stopped praying for you, hoping that God would bring you to your senses before you made the biggest mistake of your life," Wendy replied. She looked directly into his eyes and asked, "How could you even think of marrying anybody else but me, Paul Chambers?"

Paul could see the hurt in her eyes. They had just fallen back into their relationship without discussing his engagement to Constance. Paul had hoped they could just forgive each other and move on. After all, he hadn't asked her about the trip to Africa that she took years before that instigated their break-up in the first place.

Paul dropped his head back against the headrest. "That would have been a mistake, triggered by stubbornness and unforgiveness instead of love. And it would have been unfair to both you and Constance." He paused for a while and then turned to face Wendy again. "Constance and I were good friends, kind of like you and Sergio, but she wasn't the woman I was meant to marry."

"So why did you propose to her? I mean Sergio and I are extremely close, but I wouldn't marry, Sergio. I've never thought I was meant to marry anyone but you."

Paul sighed. "If I had been thinking rationally, I would have said the same thing about you. God knows how much I love you, Wendy. Only you. The thought of being without you hurts so much. But back then, when you told me you were leaving me to go to Africa, it was like you tore my heart in two and took a piece with you. I felt so angry that I couldn't stop you, and I couldn't afford to go with you. I felt so hurt that you didn't seem to care about me, or how I felt about you altering our plans—or what we used to call God's plan for our lives." He shrugged. "That just shows how little we knew about what God had in store for us."

"Well, God is always giving us choices."

"Yes, and sometimes we let anger step in the way of us making the right choice. Once Jesus touched my heart and helped me to forgive, I realized that I never stopped loving you, Wendy." He covered his heart with his right hand. "My love for you never went anywhere. I just let a whole lot of bad feelings cover it up." His voice sounded husky but sincere.

"I wish I could take back the last two and half years." Then his sense of humor took over, and he grew animated as he quipped, "Re-do. Do over. I would be married to you by now. Living with you. Making love to you and only you, Mrs. Wendy Chambers."

Wendy eyes clouded up. "We make some foolish choices sometimes."

"And do things we can never take back," Paul agreed. "That's why I praise God for keeping me, in spite of all the temptation. And I'm glad I don't have to apologize to you, Wendy. I can honestly say that when we get married, you will be my first love as well as my first lover."

"Me too. You too." She giggled. "You know what I mean."

"I'm looking forward to that night."

Paul leaned forward, so Wendy could feel his breath on her face.

"Me too," Wendy exhaled the words as Paul's lips met hers. They shared a deep, exploratory kiss.

The next day, Paul and Wendy went to the church where they grew up. Everybody was praying for the president and talking about the inauguration. When the elderly saints got up to testify, they talked about the oppression they had lived through, the racial hatred that barred them from the lunch counters and public bathrooms, and confined them to colored train cars and riding in the back of the bus. And they gave God, "Glory," that they had lived to see the election and were anticipating the inauguration of the first black president of the United States.

After the service, Reverend Walker met briefly with Paul and Wendy in his study.

"It does my heart well to see you two together again," Reverend Walker said, hugging them both.

"We made it back home," Paul replied.

Reverend Walker nodded. "And we're here to welcome you with open arms." He gestured toward two seats where Wendy and Paul could sit facing him as he sat behind his desk.

"We know your schedule gets pretty hectic, Reverend, but since we'll be heading back to school soon, we wanted to know if we could schedule our first marriage counseling appointment."

"Well now." Reverend Walker straightened his arms against the desk and leaned back peering down at Wendy's hand. He noted that he didn't see a ring on her finger.

"We're not officially engaged," Paul explained. "But, Pastor, I ain't gonna marry nobody else," Paul concluded colloquially.

"What do you say to that, Sis?" Reverend Walker asked Wendy.

"It took him long enough to come to his senses," she replied.

They laughed.

"Seriously though, praise the Lord. Hallelujah! Thank you, Jesus! And

I second that emotion. I ain't gonna marry nobody else," Wendy added laughing.

Reverend Walker nodded and looked over his calendar. "Well, I don't have to ask you how long you've known each other, or how long you've been dating, or about your backgrounds—having known you all your life. But understand Paul that we'll need to establish that there is complete closure of your other relationship."

"Yes, Pastor."

"No double dipping. No stepping in and out of relationships; no going back and forth."

"Reverend Walker, you know me better than that."

"I know you as a boy, but you haven't hung around here much for the last couple of years, so it's going to take more than words to reveal to me the character of the man you've become."

Paul nodded. "Yes, Reverend Walker. I understand."

"Wendy, are you free three Saturdays from now at about 1 p.m.?"

"Yes, Pastor," she and Paul answered in unison.

He looked unsmilingly from one to the other. "I didn't see either one of you check those electronic databases all purpose digital cell phone things that you young people carry. If I schedule you for an appointment, I'll expect you to be here."

"Pastor, we'll clear our calendars if there is anything on it," Wendy replied.

"It's that important to us," Paul added.

"Well, we're looking at one counseling session per month for at least the next six months. Exactly how soon are you children planning on getting married?"

Paul and Wendy looked at each other. Paul wanted them to get married that summer, but he hadn't formally proposed to Wendy yet. As he heard Reverend Walker use the word children, he had the sinking feeling that their pastor still thought they were too young. He hoped Reverend Walker would not suggest that they wait until they turned twenty-one.

Wendy had been so thankful that she and Paul were back together again that she had been enjoying their renewed friendship and hadn't spent much time thinking about a wedding. The fall semester had started off with Constance's big announcement that she was engaged to marry Paul. It didn't feel right to start off the spring semester proclaiming that she had gotten her man back and he was going to marry her instead. For the moment, their friendship felt just right the way it was.

"We haven't settled on a date yet, Pastor," Paul said.

"No we haven't discussed a date," said Wendy.

"Well, we can still start the counseling sessions. Counseling often uncovers other crucial issues a couple hasn't discussed. So I'll see you for counseling in three weeks."

"Thanks, Reverend Walker."

"Let me pray with you before you go." Reverend Walker thanked God for reconciling them unto Himself and unto each other. He thanked God for their parents and the village that raised them, and he asked God to continue to guide and protect them every step along life's way.

CHAPTER TWENTY-THREE

Sergio awoke to a frigid cold temperature on the morning of the inauguration. He hadn't slept much during the night, anxiously awaiting the big event. It was as though he had spent the past twenty-four hours stepping back in time, as the nation celebrated the birthday of Rev. Dr. Martin Luther King, Jr. on the eve of Inauguration Day. Forty years earlier the civil rights leader had been assassinated while spending his adult life fighting for the nation to grant black Americans the same rights and opportunities that white Americans enjoyed. The inauguration of the first African American president, elected by a majority white vote, was a fulfillment of the legacy of Rev. Dr. Martin Luther King.

The layers of clothing Sergio wore that morning did little to guard him from the sub-zero wind-chill. He wore a skull cap with another hat over it and a thick scarf around his neck, but the throng of bodies descending into the train station in the darkness of the early morning buzzed with excitement and generated their own heat. Everyone was talking to everyone, like old friends or long lost relatives reunited at a family reunion. Like an army of contented soldiers, they arrived on Capitol Hill, waited patiently and followed orders, until the sun came out and the Mall filled up with thousands of smiling faces.

Hours later, the dignitaries came into view. Those who stood too far away to see the presidential party with their naked eyes watched on the television screens that had been mounted intermittently outdoors along the Mall. Sergio and his college delegation weren't standing close enough to shake the President's hand, but they didn't have to rely on the television to see him clearly either.

Guests arrived at the hotel in Jamaica wearing strapless evening gowns, halter back dresses, and high heels. The ladies donned a shawl as a fashionable accessory, but they didn't need it to keep warm. While it was freezing cold in the United States, the weather on the island of Jamaica was characteristically warm. The men dressed in tuxedos as a formality, but some hung their jacket over their shoulder to beat the heat. After tuning into CNN that morning to join the United States and well wishers all around the world in watching the Inauguration ceremony, Jamaicans were now celebrating with their own tropical Inauguration Ball, hosted by Wendy's parents at their hotel.

Paul placed his laptop in the center of the dining table, hooked up the webcam and called Wendy's parents.

"Good evening, Mr. Douglas."

"What's good, Son?"

"It's been an exciting day," Paul observed.

"I can imagine," Devon replied. "We're overseas, but judging from the jubilation around here, you would think it's our country that has just made history. President Barack Obama is our president too."

"Did you sell a lot of tickets for the Inauguration Ball?"

"We're sold out. This is the most profitable event the hotel has ever had. I'm grateful to Troy and Tricia for coming up with this idea. So many of the people who live here are naturalized Americans like Marcia and me. Add to that the tourists and local well wishers who want to be connected with this auspicious occasion. We had a waiting list. If we had a larger venue, we would have had no problem filling it."

"Wendy and I are getting all dressed up to join you by webcam."

"Great! I positioned a camera where you'll be able to see the ballroom. We set up an enormous HDTV so our guests will be able to view the news coverage of what's happening over there all evening."

"Sounds like you have everything covered," Paul complimented him.

"Honey, could you come here for a second?" Paul could hear Wendy's mother call from the other room.

"Paul, call us back in about two hours. By then, the Inauguration Ball should be underway."

"Wait!" Paul requested. "I have a very important question to ask you and your wife."

Devon paused for a moment, not missing the serious tone of Paul's voice. "All right. Hold on for a moment. Marcia needs me in the other room."

Paul fidgeted nervously as he waited for Wendy's parents to return. His own mother was in her room resting. She planned to stay up late watching the proceedings as they unfolded on television.

"Hi, Paul," Marcia greeted him.

"Hello, Mrs. Douglas. You look beautiful. I love your hair."

"So do I!" Devon agreed, wrapping his arms around her waist as he stood behind her and kissed her on the neck.

"Devon!" Marcia gasped.

Paul cleared his throat.

"Thank you, Paul," Marcia replied. The weight she'd gained during her pregnancy made her face fuller. She chose to wear her hair out, but its sun-kissed highlights contrasted sharply with her deep tan, emphasizing her glow. "How are you?"

"Fine."

"How is your mother?"

"She's fine, too."

"Praise the Lord."

Devon whispered in Marcia's ear.

She giggled then gently pushed him away. "Behave," she told him. Then she turned her attention back to Paul. "Devon said you wanted to ask us something."

"Yes, I do. At least that's what I hope Wendy will say after I ask her to marry me tonight. Mr. and Mrs. Douglas," Paul held up the open box with the engagement ring, "May I have your permission to propose to Wendy tonight."

"Well, let's see," Devon said, feigning reluctance.

Marcia shoved him again. "Be serious, Hon," Marcia scolded him. "Paul, we've already accepted you as our son. You have our permission, but I'll leave you two to talk things over, man to man." She kissed her husband gently on the lips, and as he attempted to deepen that kiss, she pushed him away again.

As she walked away, he reached behind and lightly tapped her on the rear.

"I hope your future son-in-law didn't see that," she called out, leaving the room.

Devon turned toward the computer screen and saw Paul with his head hanging down. "Hello," he said.

Paul looked up. "I'm still here," Paul replied. He thought marriage looked real good on Marcia's parents, but he felt a little embarrassed watching them as they played around with each other.

"So, are you nervous?" Devon asked.

"Yes," Paul answered, nodding.

"Why? It's not like she'd turn you down. After all, she's been telling us for years now that you're the only guy she's ever wanted to marry."

"Do you think she'll say yes?" Paul asked.

"Do you think she won't?" Devon retorted.

"Maybe," Paul admitted.

His response took Devon by surprise. "What makes you say that?

From the first day Wendy introduced us, you've been trying to convince me that you two should marry each other, and now you have doubts. Let me guess, you two had a fight."

"No, we haven't been arguing. I'm just sorry that I was ever engaged to Constance. I think that whole episode of my life hurt Wendy more than she admits."

"Of course it did. But if she didn't love you so much, it wouldn't hurt so much. And if she hadn't forgiven you and welcomed you back, you wouldn't be together today."

"What do I do if she says no?" Paul asked.

He sounded so pitiful that Devon felt sorry for him. "Ask her again on some other day."

That simple advice caused Paul to feel relief, helping him realize that his and Wendy's future didn't necessarily rest on her response to him on that night. "Mr. Douglas, do you mind telling me what it was like when you proposed to your wife?"

"She turned me down."

"What?"

"She said she wanted to obtain her college degree first, and I should ask her again in few years."

"Oh no. That's messed up." Paul could hardly believe what he was hearing. Wendy's father always seemed so confident, and he and his wife seemed so happily married now. He asked, "How did you ever get her to change her mind?"

"I offered to pay for her college education, so she could finish faster, but knowing she wouldn't want charity, we agreed that she could work at the hotel in return."

"Wow! I had no idea."

"Well, now you know. Think about how you would feel if you were Wendy. If you love her as much as you say you do, then give her time."

"So, you don't think she'll accept my proposal tonight?"

"I honestly don't know. You'll have to ask her that."

Paul smiled. He had wanted permission from Wendy's parents and now he had it, complete with advice from her father. "Thanks, Mr. Douglas. I will call again when Wendy's here."

"Later then."

"Later."

Paul and Wendy ate dinner with his mother. The computer, tuned into the inauguration ball at the hotel in Jamaica, occupied a space at the dining table, but it was the television that commanded most of their attention.

After dinner, Paul's mother retired to her bedroom while Paul and Wendy continued their date in the living room. The evening unfurled elements of a fairytale, as the Obamas took center stage at the Neighborhood Ball in Washington, D.C. for their first dance.

Paul stood with his arms wrapped around Wendy as Beyoncé sang to the president and his wife, "At last, my love has come along. My lonely days are over, and life is like a song."

Wendy leaned back against Paul, and they swayed to the gentle rhythm of the music.

At the end of the song, Paul switched off the television and spun Wendy around to face him. "I love you so much," he said. "All of our lives together, you've already been everything to me that a husband would ever want his wife to be. You've been my best friend. You've been the joy in the midst of my sorrow. You've been my prayer partner. You've encouraged me. You've made me better than I am when I'm on my own. To use the old school Bible word, you've been my helpmeet. I praise God for you, Wendy. I can't imagine my future without you."

Paul held on to Wendy's hands and knelt down before her. "Wendy Tapper Douglas, will you allow me to change your name one more time? Will you bless me by becoming my wife?"

Wendy's eyes sparkled as her lips parted in a radiant smile. Soft laughter escaped her lips. She nodded and replied to Paul's proposal with two words: "At last."

"Thank you, God," Paul whispered as he slipped the ring onto her finger. He stood up and pulled her into his arms. Their kissed lost all gentleness and reserve, as he no longer felt the need for grid-iron restraint. He explored deeper, and tried to move closer. "For this reason a man shall leave his mother and father and be joined to his wife, and the two shall become one flesh." It was recorded in Genesis, capturing the beginning of time, and Paul looked forward to the day when those words would be manifested in his life.

"I'm going to be such a good husband," Paul said, joyously. His humor also helped them not get too heated; too tempted.

Wendy laughed. "I know you will. I love you, Paul Chambers. You are and will always be the only man I want to marry."

They kissed again.

Their bodies parted about arms length, and Wendy held up her left hand to admire her ring. The image of Constance flaunting her ring at the club fair flashed across her face.

Paul didn't miss the sudden change in her expression. "Wendy, what's wrong?"

"Nothing," Wendy replied.

She'd looked to Paul like she felt a sharp pain. "Are you sure?" He slipped his fingers between hers and held on to both her hands again.

She looked up at him.

"You don't ever need to hide anything from me," he said.

Wendy sighed. The night had been so perfect at first. The celebration; the proposal. But he was right. It didn't make sense for them to start out on the road to marriage with her hiding something that bothered her so much.

"I remembered Constance just now, at the club fair, holding up her wedding ring right after I had been talking to you, hoping we would get back together. It just brought back the pain of that moment when I first found out you were engaged to her." Wendy sniffled. Tears replaced the joyful sparkle in her eyes.

"I'm sorry," Paul said hoarsely. He hugged her tightly, then pulled back so she could see his eyes as he spoke. "I am so sorry. That was the biggest mistake of my life. I wish I had a do-over." He sighed, shaking his head. The night had gone so much better than he'd expected, until this moment.

He led her over to the sofa. She sat down, but he pulled up the arm chair, so he would be seated directly in front of her. He held both her hands and maintained eye contact. He needed for her to look into his eyes and see the love that lay in his heart and soul; a love that was hers and hers alone.

"I never told anyone this before because Constance is my friend," he paused, "as Sergio is yours. She never set out to hurt anybody. I also don't think a guy should kiss and tell. What happens in a relationship isn't everybody's business." He sighed again. "I never asked Constance Channing to marry me."

Wendy knitted her brows at him.

"I didn't. Believe me. I was going along with our relationship, enjoying the amazing success that she brought to my music career. We were good friends. Close friends even. When we were on tour last summer, she said we were so good together and brought out the best in each other, we should get married. I said okay."

Wendy blinked back tears.

"I can't explain, Wendy, why I wasn't thinking about us. I was too hard headed and unforgiving and just lost. So, I was going along with what was working in my life. Constance's mother died when she was a child, and her father let her keep her mother's wedding ring. She started wearing it on that day, and saying that I was her fiancé. I went along with it because I wasn't thinking that you and I would get back together and there was no one else I wanted to marry."

Wendy shook her head, and didn't try to check the flow of tears.

"I'm so sorry. It was foolish. It shows how weak I was. You know, I try to be a man of conviction; a man of God. I sure wasn't acting like it then. I was foolish, and I'm sorry my foolishness hurt you so much."

Wendy pulled her hands away and took off the ring.

Paul gasped. "What are you doing?"

She sniffled. "Paul, I will marry you, but I can't go back to the college wearing this ring. I can't do it. Everyone knows that a semester ago you were engaged to marry Constance. So when we return in the spring semester, and you're engaged to me..." She shook her head. "I can't do that. I can't handle the spotlight."

Paul felt like his heart had crashed to the floor. Tears burned at the back of his eyes. He couldn't draw on any humor to lighten that moment.

"Wendy, please."

"Please what? You, please be patient with me. I need some time."

A magical evening came crashing to an end for Paul. He made it through the motions of driving Wendy home and returning to his mother's apartment to clean up. In keeping with his daily routine, he got on his knees with his Bible open before he climbed into bed. He wasn't sure what to read. Perhaps, he would find comfort in Psalm 139, where he would read that God knew all about him before he was born. As he turned the pages, Psalm 121 caught his eyes: "I will lift up mine eyes to the hills, from whence cometh my help. My help cometh from the Lord, which made heaven and earth." He did find comfort in those words. He didn't control the outcome of that evening. God was in control, and Paul would continue to put his trust in Him.

"Lord Father God, Dad," Paul opened his prayer calling on God in a way that was familiar to him. His mother had taught him that although his biological father had died, his father in heaven was always with him. She told Paul he could talk to God at any time about anything, and as he read his Bible and prayed, he would hear God leading him and guiding him through life. His mother's words comforted him back then, and as he grew older, he continued to do what his mother suggested.

Paul mulled over the past few years in his mind, realizing that it wasn't until Wendy met her father in their senior year of high school that his relationship with his heavenly father seemed inadequate in helping to solve his problems. Prayer didn't change the fact that Wendy no longer seemed to need him, once she had her father and his money. The more of her father's money she spent, the greater the chasm formed separating them from each other. He relived the events of the last two years in his mind.

The two thousand dollars Wendy spent on the plane ticket to Africa drove the final wedge between them. Paul had felt hurt and helpless that he couldn't convince her to change her mind, and he lacked the resources to go with her. With Wendy gone that summer after they finished high school, Paul jumped at the chance to get away. He went ahead of Wendy to the college, where he worked retail and earned extra money as a replacement musician in a band.

That's when he met Constance. They shared a mutual love of music, and she opened the door to a recording contract and a chance for Paul to make more money.

Paul realized now that he was trying to empower himself by earning more, so he could compete with Wendy's dad, who in his mind at that time had stolen her affections because of his money. He hadn't anticipated getting so involved with Constance, whose father ironically had far more money than Wendy's father had.

Paul chuckled, finding truth in the saying that God has a sense of humor.

"Lord Jesus, I ask you to forgive me. Forgive me for losing sight of what's important in your eyes. Thank you that you never left me even though I didn't keep my eyes on you. Thank you for the songs you gave me that caused others to know and love you more. Thank you that you're a God of freewill, who allows us to make choices. Thank you for waking me up, so that I will no longer be tossed with the wind, but will consciously seek you once again to guide me in this life. Lord, thank you that you've led me back to Wendy. I pray for Constance that you will bless her with someone who truly loves her, and won't just fall into a relationship with her because of what she can do for them. Forgive me, Lord. I never intended to do that. I never meant to use her or to hurt her. I tried to be a good friend to her, but I know it would have been a mistake to marry her. Lord, I believe that Wendy is the wife you have chosen for me. Please work things out between us. Help me to get it right in your eyes. Open our hearts to the love you have in store for us. Lord, I praise your name, and I thank you and worship you, in Jesus' name. Amen."

Paul felt his sadness and disappointment diffuse to be replaced by peace of mind.

Early the next afternoon, Paul received a call from Wendy's father.

"How're you doing, Son?"

"Don't ask," Paul replied.

"That bad, huh?"

Paul shrugged, but realized Devon couldn't see him because they were using their cell phones. "Did Wendy tell you?"

"No, but the fact that she didn't call us up exclaiming that you guys got engaged tells me that she probably said no."

"It might have been better that way. She said yes, at first, and I was so happy, and everything was going well. Then she looked at the ring and started talking about Constance, and she took the ring off…" There was a catch in his voice.

"Ouch. She took the ring off. I know that hurts. So what did my daughter who doesn't want to marry anybody else but you say then?"

"That she needs time."

"Fair enough."

But life didn't seem so fair to Paul just now.

"Everything was just perfect, until she gave me back the ring," he said. "That's the ultimate rejection right there. I can't even look at the ring without feeling hurt." Paul knew he sounded like he was whining, which wasn't like him, but he couldn't help himself. He hoped Wendy's father would sympathize, having been there himself.

Devon laughed. "You'll be alright. When you're married and making babies, you and Wendy will look back at this time and smile. In the meantime, be thankful that you're living in the same state. During the years I was waiting for Marcia to marry me, we weren't even living in the same country. That, my son, was hard."

"But at least you knew how long you'd be waiting. All Wendy said was that she needed time. How much time?"

"I'll give you the same advice my mother gave me on the night I proposed to Marcia. She reminded me that some things are worth waiting for. I have no doubt that when the time is right, you will be marrying my daughter. It's not time yet, but have faith."

Paul thought of how absurd it was that Wendy's father was telling him to have faith. When they met, faith was all Paul had. He didn't have money, or a car, or a college education, or a music career, but he had faith in God. He sighed. "You're right," he told Devon. "Thanks for listening, and for your advice."

"No problem, man. Take care."

"God bless. Give my love to my future mother-in-law."

"Now that's more like it," Devon said, chuckling. "Bye."

CHAPTER TWENTY-FOUR

Paul started the spring semester with a renewed sense of purpose. He was no longer just going with the flow as he had for the last couple of years. Instead he set goals geared at laying the foundation for him and Wendy to live together as a married couple—whenever she finally agreed to a wedding. And he decided that he wanted to help heal the college community that had supported him so generously in his short-lived music career.

The start of the spring semester lacked the excitement that typically marked their return to the college campus. Like Constance, many students desired a transfer to another institution, and some returned with the attitude that they just needed to get through one more semester and they were out of there.

Wendy hadn't been involved in many social clubs and didn't interact with a whole lot of people, but even she noticed that there seem to be a damper on the college spirit. After catching up with Sergio, she came away feeling his sadness, despite his clear determination to maintain his position as student government president and complete all his course work in time to graduate in May.

"How was your day?" she asked Paul as they ate dinner together one evening.

"Good. I made the final revisions on the paper for Professor Abbey. I think it's almost as good as yours." Paul winked at her as he spoke.

Wendy smiled. She detected a spark in Paul that wasn't evident in anyone else she'd interacted with that day. Was it just his sense of humor? "It's better than you think. You've worked really hard on it."

"It's not like Professor Abbey would accept any less than our best. How is Sergio doing?"

"He's fine, physically, but he seemed a little depressed to me. You'd have to know him really well to notice. For the most part, he's fine."

Paul reminded himself not to be jealous of just how well Wendy knew Sergio. After all, he was the one that had gotten engaged to someone else. "He isn't the only one down in the dumps. I ran into quite a few people today who seemed to be walking around with a dark cloud over their head."

"I think Kane, Monique, and Sergio touched everybody's lives. I don't think we've gotten over what happened last semester. Sergio and Monique aren't the only ones still trying to heal."

"I know. The college administration wants us to sweep it under the rug and move on. I think that's going to do more harm than good."

"You're right," Wendy agreed. "What happens to a wound if you cover it up but don't treat it?"

Paul skinned up his face distastefully. "It festers and turns into a sore."

"Yup," Wendy agreed nodding. As though she'd said it all, she shut up.

Paul smiled at her as he thought about the situation. He didn't agree that they should just sit back and wait for more trouble. If no one else brought up the tragedy in a year, the media would. The media could be counted on to revisit the campus for an anniversary story aimed at uncovering how students had fared since the tragedy. They needed another type of event before then... something that would make as profound a mark on the college's image, except that it needed to be positive and uplifting.

As Paul brainstormed for an idea, he began to hum a tune and drum on the table.

Wendy recognized an old song they used to sing in church as children, but Paul added an upbeat tempo and funky rhythm. She liked it! As she bopped her head to the beat, she chimed in, "Woo, ooh, ooh," at the right moment, as she mentally followed along with the words:

"It only takes a spark, to get the fire going. And soon all those around will warm up in its glowing. That's how it is with God's love, once you've experienced it. You want to sing, it's fresh like spring. You want to carry on..."

"You're that spark," she said to Paul.

He wrinkled his brows at her.

"You are. Always. Even when we were in high school, or elementary, or whatever. You always saw the bright side of things. And if there was no bright side, you'd create one. That's one of the things I love most about you."

"Thank you very much. Thank you very much." Paul replied in a playfully husky voice.

"So what are we going to do?" Wendy asked.

"Let's have a concert," Paul suggested. "A huge hope for healing concert with all the gospel and contemporary Christian music artists who will come. We're going to fast and pray that God will use it to spark a revival on campus. To really touch hearts, and save souls, and give people a new life in Him. Like he's done for us, you know. What do you think?"

Wendy smiled at him in genuine admiration. "I think I love you," she said and kissed him lightly on the lips. She remembered how comforted she'd had felt on the night of the incident when Paul sang to her while they were waiting to hear if there were any fatalities. Music, the right music, would soothe and uplift. "So what do we do next?"

"Propose it to Sergio. Hopefully, he'll love the idea and present it to the powers that be on campus. I'll recruit Constance's help in retaining the artists. But before we talk to them, let's fast for the next couple of days and seek God's blessing on this."

"Amen."

"Amen."

Sergio loved the idea. He had been battling extreme emotions, feeling inspired by the new president of the United States, but regretful that he didn't have a family like the Obamas. He felt determined to graduate on time, but was overwhelmed by the amount of work that he needed to get done. He missed the physical intimacy of a woman, but sought instead to nurture his spirit through Bible reading and prayer.

The legacy he wanted to leave behind at the college was not the memory of one tragic evening when three students were shot and he almost lost his life. He embraced Paul's idea as a chance to create a brighter image.

"I'm new to this whole faith in God thing," he told Paul, Wendy, and Matilda as they walked over to one of the conference rooms to the first planning meeting for the event. "But I read that faith can move mountains, and that's what we need to happen tonight to get everyone on board with this event. I'm counting on you all to be the prayer wheels turning behind the scenes."

"We've got you covered," Wendy said.

Paul didn't mind that Sergio had taken control of the planning. In his position as student government president, he was the natural liaison between the students, faculty, staff and administration. They needed everyone's support, and Sergio was charismatic enough to persuade them to join in. "Let me know what you need me to do," Paul requested.

"Well, Mr. Celebrity Hot Shot, I need you, Constance, and Brad to work your entertainment magic, pull some strings, whatever it takes to get some famous gospel and contemporary Christian music celebrities here. Their names are going to draw the crowd."

"Do you have specific artists in mind?"

"I don't know them. That's yours and Wendy's music. Like you said, we need them singing songs that will uplift us, and help us pull something positive from last semester's tragedy. Songs that will unite us, and soothe the pain so many of us are still feeling."

"Especially those who were close to Kane," Wendy said solemnly.

"Have you thought about inviting his mother?" Matilda asked.

"Paul mentioned it, and that's a great idea," Sergio replied. "We'd like to show her that people cared about her son."

"Yeah, she might be in a pretty lonely place right now," Matilda said. "I mean, God forbid that we'd lost you that night, they might have named a scholarship after you or something, but Kane took himself out..." She stopped talking, overwhelmed by sadness about that night.

Sergio put an arm around her. "You see what I mean. People are still hurting, but the campus administration wants to brush everything under a rug and move on. That's not right, and I'm not about to let that happen."

"We're not about to let that happen," the others agreed.

Paul looked over at Sergio as they neared the auditorium. He admired him for this. For most of his time on campus, he'd come to know Sergio for his reputation as a player who earned good grades and possessed enough charisma to win elections. Now that he interacted with him personally, he was beginning to see another side of Sergio, the side that Wendy loved and embraced as her brother.

They walked into the conference room and were pleasantly surprised to find it filled up with students and faculty, eagerly waiting to hear Sergio's proposal.

"Good afternoon, everyone. Thanks for coming. I'm just grateful to God that I'm still here: a walking, talking, living, breathing miracle. As you know, Kane isn't so lucky, and Monique and I bear the scars from a tragic evening that many people would sooner forget, or pretend it never happened."

He paused and scanned the faces around the room. "Some people have successfully moved on, but I'll bet that the media will be back here on the anniversary to remind us of the life that was lost and the horrific circumstances of that day. I'd like to propose such a large scale event that it will shift the spotlight from our pain to our recovery. I propose that in April—giving ourselves enough leeway before graduation—the college should host a hope and healing gospel concert with any and all the celebrities we can get to come this way."

Murmurs reverberated around the room.

"Hear me out now, please. We are going to use music to bring people together, with positive lyrics to uplift our spirit and inspire us to keep on seeking that light at the end of the tunnel."

His audience expressed enough interest to ask questions. What artists would they invite? Did Paul and Constance have connections? How would they convince the celebrities to donate their time? Then there were suggestions: They needed to be careful not to offend the people who weren't Christian. The event should take place in the daytime because darkness would increase the need for security. Only members of the college community and their immediate family should be invited.

By the end of the meeting, they formed planning committees to work on the various details and to obtain the permission required to execute their plans.

Sergio hailed Wendy and Paul as they were leaving the conference room. "Holy Roller," he called out to her.

Wendy spun around and arched an eyebrow at him. "How may I help you?" she asked.

Paul followed her back over to the table where Sergio was seated. Only a few people remained in the room. "Congrats, man. That went really well."

Sergio shook his hand. "Thank you. I mean really. Thanks."

Paul shrugged. "Praise the Lord! Give God all the glory."

"That's it," Sergio agreed. "I need you guys to do your holy stuff. You know, pray, fast, whatever it is that you do when you're asking God to work a miracle."

"And just what miracle are you asking God to perform?" Paul asked.

Sergio reflected silently for a moment. "I'd like this event to draw a crowd, but be peaceful. I'd like the atmosphere to be filled with love. And I want everyone to leave there better than they were when they arrived."

"Amen," Paul and Wendy replied.

CHAPTER TWENTY-FIVE

Spring burst forth magnolia and cherry blossoms in an assortment of colors. Their pink, purple and white petals colored the atmosphere and attracted crowds who remained outdoors to bask in their beauty. During the winter months, college students bundled up and hurried to pass the bare branches of the trees which they now sat idly under enjoying the spring blossoms. This renewal, rebirth, restoration of life was especially significant after the tragedy and all that had been lost.

Graduation day approached, but in the days leading up to the concert, graduation day held the position of second priority in Sergio's mind. He felt grateful to Paul for giving him something so positive to focus on and hoped Paul really didn't mind that most people were crediting him as the visionary behind the event.

The concert started during the club hour, a time that was left free from scheduled classes, so that students could participate in the college's social clubs. They came out in droves to the field where they'd gathered in the fall for the club fair. A covered stage had been constructed this time to protect all the electronic equipment, so that rain or shine, the concert would go on. Some famous artists headlined the show, but Paul had requested that they sing songs that evoked an atmosphere of prayer. When Paul arranged the sound system for the concert, he also requested that a big screen be installed to display images and words. He planned to post the lyrics to the songs, so the audience could sing along.

The show opened with a rendition of the group 21:03's Cover Me, one of Paul's favorite songs: "Remember to pray for me, that I might go in peace... Keep my name on your mind, when you go to God next time. I need you to cover me."

The song incorporated the Bible verse on which it was based. As they sang, "The effectual, fervent prayer of the righteous availeth much," they quoted a segment of James, chapter five, verse sixteen.

In his post as student government president presiding over the event, Sergio took the microphone.

"I want to know how many of you out there are thankful that there are people covering you with prayer."

A few people in the audience clapped.

Sergio surveyed their faces and rephrased his request, "I said, I want to know how many of you out there are grateful that someone prayed for you today."

The audience responded with louder applause.

"Now that's more like it. You see, there are people covering us with prayer and most of the time, we don't even know it, much less appreciate it. I know I didn't. If you're blessed to have a praying parent, you ought to be grateful. If you've got a church family back home praying for you, you need to be thankful. And if you don't, you're still covered because somebody you know has a prayer warrior in their life asking God to bless them and their classmates, them and their co-workers, them and the people they come in contact with today—so you're covered."

Amidst laughter, the audience offered louder applause.

"I thank God for everyone out there who prayed for me—ever!" Sergio's voice became husky. "I am alive today because of you. I praise God for each and every one of you."

A hush fell over the crowd as they savored the poignant moment.

Sergio swallowed hard. "I'd like to welcome on stage two college students who I know have prayed and continue to pray for me: Wendy Douglas and Paul Chambers singing the Murrills' hit song, "God has come to heal the family."

The concert unveiled many surprise moments in which college students would be leading a song and the original artist would walk on stage and sing it with them.

Monique joined Sergio on stage, along with the entire football team, for the moment in which they would honor Kane's mother. As she approached the group, Kane's mother appeared poised and elegant in her cream colored business suit, but as she neared Monique she started yelling and name calling, blaming Monique for the death of her son.

Monique's knees buckled as she fell to the floor in tears. "I'm sorry," she sobbed. "I'm so sorry. I wish I could bring him back. I loved him too. I loved him too."

Constance walked on stage and got on her knees beside Monique, wrapping one arm around her to support her. Wendy joined her on the other side. Pretty soon, their friends and teammates, fraternity brothers and sorority sisters joined them on their knees, crying.

It seemed the sky began to cry with them as the raindrops started to fall, fat, heavy raindrops that seemed to fall one at a time. No one moved to seek shelter from the rain.

A female vocalist belted out, "Let your glory fill this place… and purify our hearts." By the time she got to the chorus of Sha' Simpson's song of praise and worship to the Lord, the audience joined in: "Rain on us. Breathe on us. Shower down… Send your Spirit, Lord."

The rain came heavier, but the congregation remained transfixed, as raindrops mingled with their tears.

Monique's parents came on stage. Her father seemed to try to hold her back, but her mother came close enough for the microphone to amplify her voice.

"I'm sorry. I see what you all are trying to do here, and it's a good thing, but I'm sick and tired of this woman blaming my daughter for her son's death."

Standing face to face, Monique's mother and Kane's mother glared at each other.

"Your daughter is nothing but a money hungry gold-digger," Kane's mother hissed.

"My daughter is far from perfect," Monique's mother retorted, her voice deep and stern, "but she did not kill your son. It is your son who tried to kill my daughter, and only succeeded in killing himself." Her eyes filled with tears as she watched the tears stream down the face of Kane's mother. "I… I'm sorry you lost your son, but my daughter has suffered enough. Please stop blaming her." She sniffled. "Please stop blaming my daughter."

Monique's father stood by his wife's side and wrapped an arm around her.

Kane's mother leaned on the support of her family and friends.

Paul nodded to Brad who stepped forward speaking the words of Jeremy Camp's song, "Healing Hand of God." The lyrics were posted, and by the time the audience began singing the chorus, many stretched their arms upward, hands reaching heavenward, as though to grasp the healing hand of God.

A female group stood toward the back of the stage and sang softly, "Forgive Me," by Rebecca St. James and Barlow Girl. The lyrics were crystal clear as piano keys played softly in the background. Many took on the personal prayer request, "Lord, forgive me, now."

Concert organizers had the local radio stations—AM 1190 and Star 99.1 on FM—to thank for the blending of gospel and contemporary Christian music. The sound might have been different and typically appealed to different listeners, but during the concert, listeners embraced each song for its message of faith, and its prayer.

Paul, Wendy, Sergio, Matilda, Brad and Constance, moved among the crowd gathered on stage, and tried to get them to stand and hold each other's hands for the next song. They lifted their voices with Casting

Crown's song, "Praise You in this Storm."

Heavy rain brought the concert to an end, but the crowd dispersed slowly, people stopped to hug and share words of encouragement and support.

Wendy couldn't wait to get alone with Paul. She praised God for him, and for the vision God had given him that had blessed so many people.

Even as teenagers, she had loved the way Paul witnessed boldly for Jesus. As they faced ridicule from their peers, they looked to each other to bolster their faith. As they prayed and read their Bible together, they were empowered time and again to praise God in their public high school, in the work place, or just walking down the street.

Individually, they had faith, but together, they were a formidable pair that God used mightily. That was the reason God had chosen Paul to be her husband, Wendy concluded. She couldn't wait to get alone with him to tell him she was ready to start planning their wedding.

EPILOGUE

Their college graduation came first, an answer to their mothers' prayers.

A year after Sergio and Constance graduated, Paul and Wendy walked down the aisle. Dressed in their cap and gown, they collected their college degrees.

Five months later, their wedding day finally arrived.

A hummingbird fluttered its wings, as it hovered and sipped nectar with its long beak from the center of a red hibiscus flower. This scene outside the Douglas residence could still be frozen in a picture frame and used to lure tourists from chilly New York to the warm, tropical weather on the island of Jamaica. Paul and Wendy used a photograph of that scene on their wedding invitations, inviting their friends and family from up north to join them for the wedding in Jamaica.

They planned the wedding for October, and although autumn temperatures made the weather in New York pleasant, other factors made the trip to Jamaica irresistible. Devon and Marcia offered some guests free accommodations at their resort; others were invited to stay for a cheap price. It was the off-season during which many rooms in the hotel typically stood vacant. The airlines offered many sales during that time, so anyone wanting to attend the wedding secured their plane ticket for a good price.

As the wedding day neared, Devon and Marcia busied themselves making preparations to host their guests. They returned home exhausted at the end of the day, on the eve of Paul and Wendy's arrival on the island. Devon parked his car, got out, opened the back door, and reached for his son in the back seat. Marcia removed the baby from his car seat and handed him over to his father.

Devon considered the baby Marcia's gift to him, a gift that had been worth waiting for. He had missed a lifetime of watching his daughter grow up, and now he prayed that he'd be there to raise his son.

He held the baby to his side in one arm, and reached out his hand to help Marcia get out of the car. He kissed her lightly on the lips as she stood beside him.

As they entered the house together, their domestic helper Dottie told them that Devon's mother was on the patio at the side of the house, behind the dining room.

"Ma," the baby said, when he saw his grandmother.

Devon chuckled. He had been there the first time his son spoke, one of many events he'd regretted missing in Wendy's life. His son said 'Dada,' and eventually he started calling everyone else, "Ma."

Marcia stuck her tongue out and made a silly face at him. She'd thought she loved Devon before she married him, but since she had gotten pregnant and had his baby, she'd grown to love him even more. He doted on her ceaselessly. While she was pregnant, he treated her like fine china—to be handled gently, so it wouldn't break. He accompanied her to every doctor's appointment, massaged her swollen feet, rubbed her back, and supplied the food to satisfy her strange cravings. He held her hand as the baby was being born. She no longer doubted how much he loved her.

They named the baby Dominique, and gave him the middle name Donovan in memory of Devon's father.

Devon sat on the floor and Marcia placed his son beside him. She walked over to Devon's mother and went over the arrangements for Wendy and Paul's wedding. Their relatives from overseas would be arriving soon. Steve, Blossom, and their daughters were staying in one of Devon's villas and had retained the services of a full-time nanny while they were there. Aunt Pat and Uncle Trevor had booked a honeymoon suite in the hotel, and Wendy and Paul were flying in the next morning.

"Marcia, look!" Devon exclaimed in a whisper.

Both women turned to face him, and saw Dominique standing. He took a shaky step forward, and then another toward Devon. Devon backed away a little and kept his arms outstretched, trying not to startle Dominique with his excitement. The baby took a few more steps into Devon arms. Devon embraced him and lifted him off the floor. He turned to face Marcia. As her eyes met his, they had a mutual understanding. This moment was a gift of God and they felt its gravity. They didn't have the power to make the miracle of love happen. They walked toward each other. Devon's mother smiled at them, treasuring her own memories as she went back inside the house.

"Thank you!" Devon told Marcia. He held Dominique at his side and embraced her.

"For what?"

"For Wendy. For Dominique." He kissed her lightly on the lips. "For loving me." He kissed her again. "For praying for me when I didn't have the good sense to pray for myself."

Marcia smiled lovingly at him. "I pray that Wendy and Paul will experience this kind of love."

"They already have," Devon said, thinking of how Wendy had forgiven Paul and given him a second chance, the same way Marcia had forgiven Devon. He knew that the forgiveness that lay in trusting the Lord Jesus was at the center of theirs and their daughter's relationship with her future husband.

In keeping with an old Jamaican tradition Uncle Trevor and Aunt Pat served as Paul and Wendy's wedding godfather and godmother. The older couple had been married for fifty years, and offered a wealth of advice and prayers.

Paul and Wendy combined the three cultures that fascinated them most and incorporated aspects of each into their wedding. They had studied enough about African customs to realize that traditions varied widely from place to place around that continent. The importance of family was a common thread, and one that the couple embraced. Paul honored his bride, as he had read that many African grooms did, by traveling to her family's hometown.

Reverend Walker and his wife made the trip with them, courtesy of Wendy's parents. He had held monthly marriage counseling sessions with the couple for the past year, and he agreed that they were ready. He stood at the altar watching Paul fidget nervously as he waited for Wendy to walk down the aisle.

The church was filled to capacity, exceeding the modest number they'd expected when they first started planning. Family and friends who had traveled from overseas with the young couple and Devon and Marcia's colleagues and local well wishers crowded into the church. An easterly sea breeze cooled the building.

Paul had participated in the wedding rehearsals, so he knew what to expect, but on the day of the wedding, it seemed like the bridesmaids crawled at a snail's pace down the aisle. Finally, he saw Wendy standing with her father by the door. "Thank you, Lord!" he said softly, but he realized that Reverend Walker heard him when he looked over and smiled. Paul cleared his throat, closed his eyes and crooned, "I just wanna be close to you," a line from BeBe and CeCe Winans hit gospel song.

Wendy's eyes filled with tears as she responded in song. Each step brought her closer to the man she'd love since he was a little boy and she a young girl. With each step, she sang from her heart looking heavenward first to her Savior, and then to her man.

About halfway down the aisle, her father had to release her arm as she sang filled with emotion that rocked her entire body and caused her to double over.

Paul took a step forward, but didn't miss a beat, singing his part in their duet with equal conviction.

"…now no one can undo I belong to you… until my dying day, I just want to be close to you."

They both extended their right arm heavenward as they sang, praising God for His love and the love He had given them for each other.

When they reached the altar, Devon bowed and held out both hands, palms facing upward, indicating that Paul was welcome to his daughter. He realized that he couldn't—not that he wanted to—stand in their way. If there was ever a marriage ordained by God, Devon felt he saw that in Paul and Wendy's relationship.

Paul grasped both Wendy's hands and held on tighter than he had in rehearsal. He closed his eyes and praised God for this day.

"I love you," Wendy said inaudibly.

Paul replied, "I love you."

Reverend Walker looked out at the congregation and said, "No closer relationship exists between two people than the love relationship between a husband and wife. It was ordained by God in creation when he told Adam and Eve, as we read in Genesis, that a man shall leave his mother and father and be joined to his wife, and the two shall become one flesh. This one flesh represents the consummation of the marriage and results in the conception of each child. It is a gift from God, and having known Paul and Wendy all their lives, I know that they are building their house on the rock of Jesus Christ."

"Amen," replied many members of the congregation.

"Dearly beloved, we are gathered here today, in the sight of God and each of these witnesses, to join Paul Chambers and Wendy Douglas together in holy matrimony."

Paul grinned from ear to ear as he said his vows. His joy was contagious causing Wendy to revert to laughter rather than tears.

Knowing how much Paul couldn't wait to get close to his wife, Reverend Walker couldn't resist teasing him a little. He said, "I now pronounce you husband and wife. You may jump the broom."

While the congregation turned to each other in surprise at the reverend's unusual declaration, Paul took one stern look at the reverend, before removing the veil from his wife's face and leaning forward to kiss her.

"…after you kiss the bride," Reverend Walker completed his statement, chuckling. He looked over at his own wife who smiled at him and shook her head.

Paul and Wendy lingered in each other's arms, savoring their first kiss as husband and wife. They needed it to be different from any kiss they'd shared before, and it was deeper, longer. An invitation to more, without the need to resist.

After many minutes, Reverend Walker cleared his throat.

The couple ignored him and remained locked in a tight embrace.

The microphone amplified Reverend Walker's voice as he whispered, "Eh hem. The sooner we end the ceremony, the sooner you get to start the honeymoon."

As Paul and Wendy stepped back from each other, they could hear laughter among the congregants. They held hands as they turned to face the congregation, took a few steps forward, and in keeping with an old African American tradition, they jumped the broom.

Their audience applauded.

Guests dined on fruit and crackers, peppered shrimp and plantains as they waited for the newlyweds to arrive at the wedding reception. They had taken a few pictures with the bridal party at the church, and on the lush tropical grounds of the resort before excusing themselves to go change for the reception. More than two hours later they hadn't returned.

Donna and Kim speculated as to the reason for the newlywed's tardiness as they got ready to perform a liturgical dance.

"I don't think they'll ever show up," Donna said. "As long as they have been waiting for some good loving."

"Girl, who you telling," Kim agreed, in strong African American sister-to-sister vernacular. "That's what I call worry free loving. You know they ain't been with nobody else."

"They ain't been with no one. Period," Donna corrected her. "I have never known another couple where both the guy and the girl were virgins on their wedding day."

"Virgins no longer. You know my man is up there in that hotel room knocking boots!" Kim suggested, lifting and lowering her shoulders as she laughed.

"I know that's right."

By the time Paul and Wendy arrived at their wedding reception, the bridal party was already seated at the head table, and dinner was served. The deejay announced their arrival.

"All rise and give a resounding welcome to Mr. and Mrs. Chambers!" As everyone applauded, the more crude among them whispered that there might already be a baby on the way.

Paul and Wendy took their places at the head table where they were immediately served dinner. They fed each other. Paul felt famished, but he took the time to savor each bite, just as he had taken his time to please his wife in the intimacy of their bedroom. They had arrived at the climax of their evening earlier than intended, but they felt fulfilled. Totally satisfied! And now they could linger at their wedding reception and thoroughly enjoy the night.

*****THE END*****

ABOUT THE AUTHOR

Shauna Jamieson Carty is a born-again Christian who writes fiction and non-fiction to show how people are strengthened to endure life's toughest situations when they trust in God who loves us so much that He gave us JESUS. Born and raised on the island of Jamaica, she began her career as a writer while living in the United States, where she earned a Master's degree in journalism from Columbia University and a Bachelor's degree in political science from Lehman College. She has edited her mother's books, co-authored a book with her husband, and encourages their children to also write and publish their work.

NON-FICTION BOOKS

Praying in the Moment: Reflections on the Election of President Barack Obama, by Shauna Jamieson Carty, spans the generations. Eight of the reflections are told through the eyes of Americans who have experienced race relations at its worst, but have now lived to witness progress beyond many of their expectations. The ninth reflection documents the experience of a young adult who attended the inauguration. The tenth gives voice to three children under age ten who express how they feel about the election of America's first black president.

By Faith: A Marriage Building Devotional with prayers, activities, and discussion topics, by Ricky and Shauna Carty, conveys the perspective that a lasting, happy and faithful marriage is a gift from God for which we should glorify Him, and not a direct construction of man for which we should credit ourselves. It can be used as an individual or couples' devotional, or it can be a workbook for married couples whereby they can record their own stories and store keepsakes as a legacy of the Christian marriage for younger generations.

Made in the USA
Middletown, DE
14 January 2022